PROFANE ALTARS

Weird Sword & Sorcery

Edited by Sam Richard

CONTENTS

INTRODUCTION
SAM RICHARD

Sword & Sorcery is just one of those genres that has been a part of my life for as long as I can remember. I guess it stems from being born in the early 80s, when the post-Conan wave of films were coming out and my dad didn't particularly care if what we rented from the video store was particularly age appropriate. *Beastmaster*, *Deathstalker*, *Ladyhawke*, *Red Sonja*, the aformentioned *Conan*, *Conquest*, hell even *The Black Cauldron* were all essential movies of my childhood. Those vibes stuck in my head at an early age and never really left.

And then came high school and finding the writing of Robert E. Howard. And then Karl Wagner and Manly Wade Wellman. More recently I've been trying to read more of the genre, with Tanith Lee, Lin Carter, and Michael Moorcock leading the charge. It's become a bit of an obsession.

Maybe it's strange for Weirdpunk to do a Sword & Sorcery book given our typical output, but that's kind of the point for me. S&S is in my DNA as much as Croneberg, the Dell Abyss titles, DIY punk, transgressive literature, and cosmic horror. If you read these stories, I think it'll makes sense.

In the spirit of prior 'smaller' Weirdpunk anthology projects (*Feral Architecture, Cinema Viscera, Beautiful/Grotesque*), the idea for this project came from a conversation. This time with friend, amazing writer, and fellow widower Charles Austin Muir. Somehow we got talking about S&S (I had just written a couple stories in the genre, the first of which is in *Forbidden Futures #12* and the second is in *Castle Jackal #5*) and expressed interest in doing more. Charles has also been a longtime fan, and from that conversation the seed of *Profane Altars* was sprouted.

Then I asked around to some mostly horror writing friends to see who else likely loved the genre and not surprisingly, all of them did and wanted to be a part of the project. It grew a little from there and now you're holding it in your hands.

It was important to me that the cover reflect the book. That it feel like something you could have pulled off a shelf at a bookstore back in the mid-70s or so. After digging around I found the cover painting. Originally a Solomon Kane 'The Right Hand of Doom' companion painting from legendary artist Jeffrey Catherine Jones. Frazetta once called Jones, "The greatest living painter," just so you know what kind of pedigree we're dealing with.

As I looked through her art and tried to find a contact for who owned her artistic estate, I learned more about her and her life. Jeffrey Catherine Jones had a prolific career as not just the painter of an enormous quantity of science fiction and fantasy book covers, but also had a long, celebrated career in comics, which included work in *Eerie, Creepy, Vampirella, Heavy Metal,* and *The Savage Sword of Conan.* In the late 70's, she shared the almost mythically legendary art space The Studio with Bernie Wrightson, Barry Windsor-Smith, and Michael Kaluta. She came out as trans in the late 90s and continued to do art on and off, mostly focusing on expressionism and later landscapes.

Jeffrey Catherine Jones died in 2011. And we remember her for the legend, pioneer, and rad human she was. And it is an amazing honor to have her art adorn the cover of this book.

The other cover elements are an homage to the Ballantine Lovecraft/Derleth titles of the mid-70s. Books which were my introduction to not just Lovecraft and Derleth, but cosmic horror as a whole when I found them at a thrift store in my early teens. My hope is that this serves to visually bridge the gap between the Sword & Sorcery and horror elements of the book.

Massive thanks to contributors Emma Alice Johnson, Adam Smith, Matthew Mitchell, Sara Century, Charles Austin Muir, and Edwin Callihan who literally made this book what it is. Additional thanks to Edwin for help with brainstorming the title, which led us to *Profane Altars*.

A huge hug and thanks to Samantha Kolesnik, who was digging in the dirt with us on this project and helped spurn it along. Eternally grateful for her friendship.

Eternal thank Mike Phillips of From Beyond Press for helping me get in touch with Jeffrey Catherine Jones' family. And then even more especially thanks to her daughter for allowing us to use one of JCJ's fucking incredible paintings for the cover.

Finally, and most of all, thank you for reading this book. I hope you like what we all conjured for ya.

TWO MOTHERS
EMMA ALICE JOHNSON

"I've brought far fiercer creatures to their end," Lorai said, braiding her fine curls into a single silver rope that hung over her shoulder.

"The dents in your metal attest to that." Feef, her armorer, kneeled before her, strapping the tarnished greaves to her shins. They felt heavy and hard against her skin, their coldness penetrating her woolen hose. How long had it been since she'd donned them?

Feef stood and reached for the heaviest cuirass in her collection.

"No, the one on the far side, Feef." Five chestplates hung from pegs on the wooden wall of her armory. Lorai pointed at the gleaming, undented one.

Feef retrieved the chosen plate. "This is a showpiece."

"And I will show it today."

She raised her arms and Feef placed it on her.

"I see your eyes, old friend." She wiggled into the cuirass, let the heft of it settle against her breasts. "You've never given me that look when arming me."

"It's been some years." He turned away, picked through a pile of mail. "Perhaps…"

Before he could finish his suggestion, she cut him off with a wave of her hand. She knew what he was going to say: perhaps someone else could go, one of the villagers. But they numbered less than a hundred. She could name every one, from the oldest to the babies now gone, the reason for this quest. "They aren't warriors, Feef."

"You've seen that they don't have to be." He held up a hood of chainmail.

She nodded. "I have fought."

Feef placed the hood over her head, adjusting it carefully so it sat just right. It was good mail, good armor, good weapons. Nobody within many days ride could claim better.

After a pause, her armorer said, "I worry who will fight when you cannot."

"Do you think I'm not coming back?"

He put his calloused hands on her shoulders and looked into her auburn eyes, his confidence back, and in sufficient quantity to share with her. "No. You will make short work of this creature."

But there was a waver. Lorai barely caught it, but she did, and it made her wonder if he had ever truly believed in her or if he had always put on a show like this. She tossed the thought aside. Her memories of victory provided all the proof she needed. She didn't lose battles. That was the truth. The silver in her hair didn't change that. The wrinkles rippling through her skin didn't change that. The ache in her joints didn't change that.

"Thank you friend," she said.

Her armorer held her shoulders a moment longer, then left the room.

She took a tentative step, letting the weight of her protection sink onto her. It had grown heavier since last she donned it, she was sure. Never mind though. She had exercised daily, lifting heavy stones, sparring with Feef. Her muscles still bulged even though her skin hung looser over them. Armor always felt heavy with the first steps, then its weight would become her weight and she would move as if not wearing it at all.

Lorai chose her sword and then there was only one last thing to do. She kneeled before a row of diminutive suits of armor, the smallest no higher than her chest even with her knee on the ground. She bowed her head, begged forgiveness of the emptiness inside of them.

Then she stood and exited the armory into the moonless night. Feef met her outside with her horse. No more words were exchanged, only the reins. Feef put down the stepping stool. Lorai climbed it and her armorer guided her onto the back of her big brown mare. The horse whispered a neigh and they were off, trotting out of the village and toward the woods.

Lorai loved these woods. Even knowing what had taken residence within them and what it had stolen, she could not feel anything but joy inside these woods. As her time passed, she spent more and more of it here, looking at every little thing, enjoying the tug of her hair caught in brambles as she walked, lifting rotten logs to watch the centipedes scurry.

Now, despite her dedication to her quest, she longed to leap from her horse and run her fingertips over the ferns, their fronds still bright green even in this time of brown. The season of berries had passed and snow would fall soon, but she could still taste the sweet fruit on her tongue as she rode through the coils of raspberry vines.

Village children often followed her out here on warm days when she came to forage. They only wanted to play battle with her though, and she always conceded. That was who she was to them, their warrior, not their berry collector. Their mothers could do that just as well as Lorai.

But now these woods were taking babies, as those

mothers put it. "It's the woods," they whispered to Lorai. "The woods." Six babies gone in as many nights. There were no more to be taken, but two on the way. Lorai knew the woods hadn't taken them, but something in the woods. She had sent her keenest man to watch. He had come back in tears, barely able to describe what he'd seen. Whatever it was, it needed a sword in its throat. There would be no more babies stolen from her village. Lorai would see to that.

She reached the clearing as the first fingers of light clasped the horizon to pull the sun up into the sky for the day. Lingering at the edge of the woods in wait for more brightness, she dismounted the horse with less grace than she'd have liked. She wasn't scared. She was tired though, it was true. Her body had gotten used to sleeping through the night. But the creature hunted in darkness and her man had seen it always return to its lair well before dawn. Lorai counted on catching it tired and settling into sleep so she could easily free it from its wretched life.

She leaned against a tree. The weight of her armor rattled loose the brown leaves that remained in its branches. They weaved through the air around her before settling onto the ground beside her sabatons. This armor. It was heavier, she swore it. All the sooner to get this over with.

The sun fully out now, she stepped out of the woods, leaving her mare behind. She'd make the remaining journey on foot. It wasn't far. She could see the pile of rubble even now, the sun lighting it up.

As she walked, she was thankful for her man who, despite his fear, had followed the creature here. There'd been a time when she had to do that labor herself. Hunt the enemy. Battle the enemy. Kill the enemy. But her record of victory bolstered people to help her, and now she could always enlist someone to do the hunting for her. All they did was point her toward what needed to be killed and she killed it – wild beasts, traitorous generals, bloodthirsty kings. Armies had fallen before her.

She thought of Feef's lack of confidence and laughed to herself. Lorai didn't lose. This was known, not just in her village, but throughout the land. She had once lost her sword and her men in battle, but still left her enemies bleeding and broken in a fury of fists and a headbutt that cracked their commander's forehead open. And Feef thought she'd fall to a creature so pathetic, so cowardly, it had to sneak into the village at night to steal babies from sleeping mothers?

The walk from the woods to the ruins took longer than expected. Lorai's body slowed against her will before she reached the halfway point. Her hips ached from lifting her armored legs. She felt as if she'd been trudging through three feet of snow. Shedding the greaves and cuisses, she told herself their clattering would not do. She'd be as well off with bells dangling from her silver braid. She still had her chestplate, but stealth and speed would be her best protection for this mission.

She pulled a bundle of salve from her pouch, dipped two fingers in it, reached her hand under her woolen hose and rubbed it into her hips until the pain broke up. Feeling a strain developing at the base of her skull, she peeled off her hood of mail, placed it next to her other discarded armor, and rubbed a bit of the unguent onto the back of her neck. Then she resumed her walk, faster and quieter now.

Even with the sun up, a tingle of cold persisted in the air. The absence of birdsong hung heavy around her. Had they already retreated from the impending snow or had the creature driven them away? Come to think of it, the woods had been unusually quiet. Well, she would solve that problem too.

Soon, Lorai stood before the ruins. They had been a castle once, in the high days, before the wars. There were no castles now, only rubble and what had been built over it. Maybe there would be castles again, though she hoped not. To her, castles only symbolized wealth unshared. She'd never understood the hoarding of treasure and power, the ability of those men – and they were all men – to look out on the starving and suffering and not see the wrongness of it. Oh, she'd tried it on for size. Even now her home was the largest in the village, the warmest, the most well-appointed. She ate good food and drank the best mead. Won battles brought riches. She'd learned to push them away eventually.

But then the villagers had come with different gifts. When they'd discovered she was baron, they'd given her their own children. Reward for her protection, they'd insisted. And when one was lost they'd come with another, mothers draped in hurt and sincerity and a desperate need to know they would always be safe. They could have more babies, they'd reasoned, as long as they were safe.

Lorai had housed the children. She'd fed them and fought them. She'd put swords in their tiny hands and fought them, again and again, each one more intensely than the next, in hopes they would beat her one day, because if they could beat her, they could beat anyone. But they never did.

Now she moved through the ruins. Underfoot, grass weaved through broken brick and fallen beam, camouflaging them, but it was all here, enough rock and wood to build a tower ten times bigger than any home in the village and just as wide. Oh the shadow it must have cast, forcing everything around it into darkness. What a waste. What a win that it had been destroyed.

Lorai had been a child during the wars, but she'd been thrown into them nonetheless. She could barely remember being taught how to fight, only being handed sword and shield and pointed in the direction of the enemy. If only her adopted children had taken to violence like she had, perhaps her home wouldn't be so cold.

She kicked through the detritus until she came to what looked like a sliver of night that held on despite the rising sun. Longing for a torch, she dipped a toe inside and watched it sink, counted the seconds until it touched the first step of many leading down into the earth. A torch would only signal her coming though, and her night vision was still strong. She'd be able to see well enough once she got acclimated, and if not she had other senses to rely on.

Touch for one. She stretched her arms out beside her, pressing her fingertips against the walls on either side of the steps, dragging them over the bricks as she lowered herself one step at a time. She paused frequently to listen but heard naught but the occasional chirrup of an insect. As she descended, her body cast the faintest shadow. Eventually that shadow disappeared as she moved further from daylight and the darkness became complete.

Her knee popped, a cracking sound like a nut being opened. She froze and in the silence that followed a sense of mirth arose at the thought of reaching her finale because of old joints that couldn't keep quiet. But no, she had not been heard. The crack may have been confined within her own skin for all she knew, echoing up her bones to her eardrums without bothering to radiate outward.

She reached a point where she could step down no further. Dragging her fingers over the walls still, she moved forward, a little faster now that she'd reached the bottom, but not much. The ground could drop away. There might be something in her path. She couldn't run headlong into this battle. She'd never been the type for that anyway, which was certainly why she still lived. Reason first; rage second. That was her mantra.

Eventually she realized she could see in front of her, and not because her eyes had adjusted. A glow emanated from somewhere ahead, faint still, but enough for her to see the chips in the mortar of the walls she passed her fingertips over, to see the rats running silently alongside her, their own missions to attend to. The glow took on a purplish hue as it brightened, brilliant when she reached its source – streams of purple liquid running through troughs on either side of the tunnel floor, which soon transitioned from flagstone to dirt, the dirt of deep earth. She wondered how far down she'd gone, into what realm she'd passed.

Lorai kneeled down to look closer at one of the streams. It moved slower than water, viscous stuff that fought over itself to get to its destination first. She ventured a fingertip toward it but stopped suddenly upon seeing a rat leap in, disappear beneath the surface for a moment before reappearing with a squeal as it's flesh dissolved from its bones.

A chill spread across the skin under her chestplate and she stood. Truly she was in the dwelling of a creature of darkness. She'd been to many such places before, but not quite like this. For one, it didn't reek of death, singed rodent notwithstanding. No rot. No stench of decaying meat. If anything, it smelled clean. Perhaps this violet muck cleansed the death from the air.

She continued on, the glowing streams her guides. They led her to a chamber. The walls here were built of solid earth and she knew she was further than the architects of the fallen castle had intended their structure to go. But the debris had been put to use, bricks and boards refashioned into furniture, a table and shelves filled with root vegetables, gourds and casks.

And more. The same materials had also been used to construct six cradles, evenly spaced, a row of three on each side of the chamber, carved bones as flourishes. A mockery of a nursery. Lorai walked between the rows. She gripped the ivory rail of one of the cradles. She dragged her fingers through the straw inside and they landed on something, a carved wooden teething ring speckled with bite marks.

The faces of the stolen babies flickered in her mind's eye, except it wasn't the stolen babies she was seeing at all, it was her babies, her children, her little fighters who had no fight in them and should never have been given to her, should never have been taken by her and never taken into battle with her. But she had taken them, and she had loved them, but not enough, not nearly enough.

But not these! She had given them up for dead. Everyone had. Creatures did not steal babies in the night only to keep them, to tuck them in and see to their warmth. Lorai had never heard of such a thing in all her years, in all her battles. Good fortune though. She'd be able to bring these little ones home. She saw herself, returning to the village, six sweet babes in her strong arms, sleeping against her bosom, one awakens and cries, clings to her, wanting to stay with her.

Lorai inspected the shelves: squash, sunchokes, heaps of black walnuts and hazelnuts, more. A bounty! Had the creature stolen these from the village too? Certainly a loss of this size would not go unnoticed. Perhaps it was gathering them itself. The thought crossed her mind of the creature growing the vegetables in a garden near the ruins, harvesting them. No, not the creature her man had described. Not the nightmare that brought him back pale and shaking. It wasn't possible.

Lorai lifted a cask from a shelf and looked inside, half expecting blood or more of the purple muck, but before her eyes even recognized the liquid, her nose did. The sweet scent of honey. Lorai ventured the tip of her pinky inside, dipped it and tasted. She'd never had such brightness on her tongue. She opened other containers and found mashed gourds, nuts ground to paste – food for babies.

Fury rose up in her. This abomination, this play at motherhood made her sick. She put the containers back on the shelf, turned and lashed out, wanting to knock over the nearest cradle, to smash it underfoot. She stopped herself from destruction that would surely wake the creature wherever it slept. Instead, she clenched her teeth and drew her sword. She'd end this perversion now and for good.

Lorai exited the nursery at the opposite end she'd entered, into another tunnel. She walked fast but quiet, putting the weight of each step on her toes. The earth was her ally here, taking each footstep in silence. A new chamber opened before her. She pressed her back to the dirt wall and sidestepped as close as possible to the opening while still hidden in the shadows. She listened, sniffed. Nothing. No wait, the gurgling voice of a baby. The creature was in there and it had the babies.

There was no time for tact, no time for strategy. The creature had not heard her, had not come for her. Lorai still had surprise on her side, and that was all she'd need. Surprise and a sharp sword had won her many battles.

She stepped into the chamber, sword poised to strike. Pools of bubbling purple muck dotted the dirt and rock floor. Her quarry hid in the corner, perched in a nest of straw, its entire body wrapped up in veined wings the color of night, head tucked in. Even curled up and crouched like this, Lorai could tell the creature was massive. It didn't move though, didn't react to her presence at all, merely rocked gently on its heels as if comforting itself.

No, not comforting itself. The coos of babies came from within those wings. It was rocking them to sleep. They didn't sound harmed. They didn't even sound scared.

Lorai knew the sound of scared babes all too well, and this was not it.

Lorai moved closer and still the creature remained oblivious to her presence. Could this be so easy? But alas she couldn't strike, not with the creature clutching the babies like this. She had to know where they were before she could drive her blade in or she'd risk skewering them too.

She puffed her breath, hoping to attract the creature's attention, but it kept rocking in silence. Was it ignoring her? Did it know she was here and think it could wait her out? Or had it truly not noticed her arrival? She wanted to lean in and shout at it, but now was not the time for rage. Not yet.

Instead, she clicked her tongue as loud as she could and settled into a fighting stance, feet hip distance apart, her sword pointed out in front of her, both hands on its hilt. Finally, the creature lifted its head, gazed at her with eyes that smoked as if made of smoldering coals. A demoness, Lorai now saw, with pale green skin and ivory horns that curled from shoots of black fur on the sides of her head.

The demoness stood, towering over Lorai, unfurled her bat wings to reveal six babies, suckling at six naked breasts, cradled securely against her body by six arms crisscrossed around them. She tilted her head curiously at the warrior woman who had come to slay her.

Lorai saw in the demoness's eyes, baron like hers, her heart wanting nothing more than to be a mother despite the rest of her body telling her she could not be. But this one had the strength to take what she desired, not to simply wait for it to be dropped at her doorstep in pity.

Lorai shook the thought away. This demoness had no claim to those babies. A desire was not a right, and those babies had true mothers back in the village who wept for them. True mothers. Lorai raised her sword and pictured the edge sheering through the demoness's neck, a vision that would come true with but a single swing, for the demoness put up no guard, her only flex of muscles to pull the babies tighter to her bosom, to protect them, not herself.

One of the babies peeled its lips from breast and hissed at Lorai. With that hiss Lorai remembered the cries of her adopted children as they fell in battle against enemies far too strong, one after the next, and she knew these babies were safe, that this mother would teach them how to survive in this world better than any other mother could, that they would grow up strong and able to defend them-selves against any opponent. No baby could hope for more.

The demoness reached one arm out into the open space Lorai's sword should have been swinging through, and with a silent flick of a razor claw opened the skin of Lorai's throat that should have been protected by the hood of mail left in the clearing outside.

Lorai's sword hit the dirt floor with a thud and Lorai followed it, quickly, as if pulled there, flopping face down, her cheek warm in the blood that drained from her faster than the earth could absorb it. With her last bit of strength, she flipped onto her back to see the demoness leaning over her. The babies now turned from their meal to watch the life drain from the fallen warrior, learning the lesson Lorai had never been able to teach.

MAYBE JUST US

ADAM SMITH

I. A BATTLEFIELD BIRTH

Ella sat on his left knee, the handle of the axe in one hand with its blade rested over his thigh. It caught the morning light and Ella thought others might find themselves distracted by the splintered sun or reflection of clouds that lazily moved across the steel he had polished the night before with beeswax and immature green leaves. The fingers of his other hand pushed down in the grass and mud, toes curling in his boots ready to launch himself into the fray ahead of him.

He would wait until the axe was needed.

Until *he* was needed.

Only then would Ella charge to Sir Davies Crookedneck.

The knight stood in the shin-high grass, its claymore shaped blades becoming drenched in the dark, red blood of the pagans fool enough to defy God and surrounding the Haloed Knights. Taller than them all, Sir Davies Crookedneck thrust his spear into the chest of the heathens, letting God and daylight inside each and every one.

Until the spear broke. No matter the finish, secreted anal glands of beavers or oil peeled from otter's fur, all wood broke from the leverage of righteousness against sinner. Their bones would chip and splinter until the small bits wormed their way toward the internal organs and flooded the corrupters' lungs in blood. The bodies' insides would inevitably wear down the weapon's finish. Until each thrust, twist, and violent pull from flesh soaked the wood like teenagers skinny dipping in the moonlight. Then the long spear would splinter along its grain, and snap. Leaving Sir Crookedneck defenseless save a broken bit of wood wrapped in batwing leather. Which Ella knew was still formidable enough to stave off any miscreant or barbarian until his squire arrived.

That is when Ella would run.

Before he had been brought into the holy knights' fold, Ella had been a circus performer. His family a troupe unto itself that traveled the kingdom, working for spare coin donations while they stole the heavyset purses that hung fat and unused from silver inlaid belts. Ella worked trapeze and drew the attention of the crowd when he let his sweaty fingers slip from the bar that swung thirty-five hands in the sky. Then he would let himself bounce from the safety net made from tattered rags and the elastic bark of Nelly trees. While the rich did their best to appear concerned and hovered above the boy playing heel in the dirt, the thieves would bleed the leather pouches of every gem and relic they carried merely to be known to carry.

In Luker Bay, the family had been found out but the idea of them being simple thieves was too alien, too unfathomable. When it was posited by Sir Davies Crookedneck and his band of Haloed Knights the family was in fact in service of Turpin, the Pagan God of Travellers and

Highwaymen, the townsfolk finally found an excuse to forgive their ignorance and ego.

Before the troupe was bound by their ankles to the masts of ships that bobbed in the harbor like leaves bound to thin limbs, Sir Crookedneck offered reprieve to all – bound themselves to their Lord, Slitneck instead. Feel his grace against their cheeks and the warm pounding of his heart from against their own chests.

To the boy, grace and heart sounded better than pratfalls, constant internal bruising, and rotten vegetable sacks as a bed while they traveled from town to town, never safe enough to stay in one village longer than three days.

All refused, save Ella. He heard their gargled screams as the tides rose. *Drowning words,* Sir Crookedneck had said while they watched from the pier, *are always lies. One last spit unto our faces and our Lord's.*

Ella took to the routine of squire work quicker than most. He managed to learn how to sharpen blades, tighten chainmail, and tan leather easily – the faith however, came slower. He still rose early and bowed his head along with the rest but never felt grace along his cheek or a heartbeat against his breast.

Except with Sir Davies Crookedneck. Faith in God or not, Ella found piety with the Knight.

That devotion carried to the battlefield. With axe in hand, he launched from his stance by the tents and saddled battle elk toward Sir Crookedneck. The long blades of grass were paintbrushes soaked in the blood of the wretched. They cut swathes of crimson red and splattered spilled pig pink colored bits of intestine against the boy's boots.

Heavy on his left side, Ella felt the world crumble and scream beneath his feet as he brought the axe to his Lord. His smile was jubilant and forced his cheeks to make way for a mouth filled with too many teeth. Ella slid to a stop on his knees, head bowed, axe outstretched over his palms. He felt the graze of Sir Crookedneck's chainmail over his fingers when the knight snatched the axe, then quickly dug the blade into the throat of an oncoming heretic, just below the heathen's jaw. A dam of splintered bone and ripped flesh let loose blood and most of a tongue that spilled onto the man's armor, and covered their blasphemous sigils in righteous viscera.

Ella did his best to not stare in awe at the monolith of death and redemption. The man was even more brutal without the distance of a spear. The axe dislocated joints with its weight then found every exposed bit of skin to maim and tear.

Sir Crookedneck had told Ella the deniers worshiped some sort of fish. An ancient and tentacled thing that lived amongst the coral and sang to the passing ships. Its song was full of lies, Sir Crookedneck had said.

Ella thought the knight heard many lies. That was maybe the cost of knowing, he thought. Or at least the cost of faith.

The cost of blasphemy to Haloed Knights was always death. Be their trespass, an offhand remark, or the destruction of an idol. All who challenged their faith were deemed damned, and Sir Crookedneck unfailingly told Ella the damned need to return home.

Ella found himself in awe each time Sir Crookedneck swung his axe to deliver the heathens. But there was one, dressed in a darker green armor than the rest who hobbled up from the mud with grit and heresy. He dug his trident into the mud and pulled himself toward the knight's back. Sir Crookedneck was reverent in his swings, each leaving a swathe of blood in the blade's wake.

Unable to stand on one leg as his left hung by stretched skin and a few straps of green dyed leather, Ella watched the man pull the trident from the mud before he thrust it toward the knight's back. Ella panicked, a squire was supposed to only serve the Haloed Knights, never act as one.

Instead, with all the faith he could muster – not in God or Halos, Ella lifted one broken end of the spear and charged toward the limp fish worshiper. The splintered end went through his left cheek, then out his right eye. The burst ocular balloon still had flecks of the man's green eyes, the rest was pink and off white.

"Ella," Sir Crookedneck said, "What the fuck have you done?"

Ella's breath made him think of the drowning voices. The lapping water that fell into their mouths and pooled in their throats. "I…"

Ella stood, the spear still in his hand on the back end, the heretic's neck twisted and still at his feet. All the knights along the battlefield, including Sir Crookedneck and the blasphemers, dropped to their knees in front of the squire. "I was only trying to help."

The violence of clashing weapons and ideology ground to a halt. Then, a loud sob burst from them all just before Ella's world went dark.

II. DIMINISHING YEARS

The sharp Halo refracted the torchlight of the church under Ella's whetstone. The Mississippi River water the squire had carried along the bank in clay jugs inlaid with rings and stone claws shimmered chimney red and dandelion yellow as it dripped off the razor-sharp steel onto the floor.

It was all there was to do until Sir Crookedneck returned.

The boy was lost, the blood of the heretic dried like a scab over his leather boots. The squire, unsure if he could even call himself that anymore, had no idea what would happen after his murder on the battlefield.

All he could do was wait – hope to be found by Sir Davies Crookedneck again.

The door opened roughly, enough that it startled Ella. The stone slipped from his hands, leaving his exposed palm to run along the halo when he twisted to look over his shoulder. The blood came slow at first, just a feeling of sharp wet. When Sir Crookedneck sat in the pew opposite Ella, he kept his head forward toward the altar. Ella's eyes stayed focused on the knight, his bloody hand resting on his lap.

"You're getting blood on my halo, Ella," Sir Crookedneck said, his voice rich with mulch and honey. "And too soon at that."

Ella picked up the cleaning mail, small rings laced together with Elk intestines that dried and gave a sweet shine to the ornate headpiece. "Sorry, sir."

"Much to be sorry about today," he rested his bare hand on Ella's shoulder. "But not that."

"Are the others angry?"

Ella had never known Sir Crookedneck to soften words, "Aye." Tonight was no different.

The squire shook his head, remembered the circus and being forced to fall again and again while his family feigned concern and cut purse from belt. His eyes followed the Knight's arm to a warm face that assured him all concern was earnest. "Are you angry?"

"I'm alive."

"And I'm glad for that but," Ella said while he attempted to wipe the blood from his hand to his pants. "I know that squires aren't allowed to-"

"Tie that off," Sir Crookedneck said. He held out a long yellow scarf with green filigree for the boy to take. "Rules of war are a strange thing.

"Folks trying their hardest to murder one another, for their own creed and purpose, but then demanding our conduct be beholden to the laws of man. While I can understand that-"

Sir Crookedneck nodded to the altar, "The Haloed Knights would never abide by just the creed of man while our God rests upon his throne."

"So it'll be them that decides what happens to me now?"

"You're a good squire, Ella," Sir Crookedneck stood. "But you are shit for piety.

"We all hoped your faith would come eventually, and I still hold fast it may, but our God only judges the haloed."

The knight bent at his knees, he somehow seemed more intimidating outside of the anonymity of his armor. There was no uniform for him to blend in with, just scars and split knuckles exposed by his plain overalls. A choker of brass tight around his unshaven neck had a track that ran its circumference where the halo locked in during battle, giving all the knights the visage of Angels. Here in the church, blood-soaked scarf around his hand, Ella thought this was the most angelic Sir Crookedneck ever appeared.

"Come boy, make sure my halo is sharper than you've ever made it. There's a long trek to make tomorrow."

Ella nodded, then kept to his word the next several hours. The rings of the knights were fashioned from Giant's bones. They had walked the Earth before the Haloed appeared. The Knights found them ungodly and slayed them all. Not wanting even their skeletons to find rest, the First Haloed fashioned the bones into iconography, weapons, and armor. At least that's how the books had been written – whether Ella believed them or not.

To him, the halos appeared to be nothing more than fine sharpened silver, or perhaps a rare rock. Maybe, he thought, this was the lack of piety Sir Crookedneck had spoken of. He rushed the thought from his mind, then set forth another hour sharpening each side until his fingers blistered and he was left with just the nub of a whetstone.

The sun was slithered to its rise like a predator in the wings, soft light beginning to breach the stained-glass windows of the church. Ella plucked one long hair from his head, held it by its end with his thumb and forefinger and flicked it against the halo. There was no sign of the cut, no force or abrasion, just a black strand of hair half its former length. He flicked the shorter strand against the inside of the halo to the same result. Content with his work, he wrapped the halo in its cleaning mail and made his way to the coming morning.

Outside, a group of tramps, all too familiar in their existence but not any tangible memory, were huddled together over a wooden crate of glass bottles, one of which they passed back and forth.

"Hey boy," one with a thick mustache shouted. He extended the bottle out to Ella and there was a comfortable scent in both the tramps and yellow spirit. Botanical and rich with minerals like a river after the rain, Ella remembered nights like this with the circus. A bathtub filled with alcohol steeped thick with stolen flowers and herbs, the way their laughs sounded in the cramped space.

Then, the running when they were found out, the high stepping over the dead bodies of whatever family that owned the house just before they spilled into the alleys and marked another village off their map as unreturnable.

"Come sit with us a while," another said. Her hair soft like a pin cushion streaked with purples and yellows. "We know ye, yeah?"

Ella tucked the wrapped Halo under his arm, began to walk away. "I don't think so."

"Oi, yeah we do. You were one of 'em swingin' kids from the Mirror House."

He hadn't heard the words together in years, their conjunction immediately put him back on the pier, the bound bodies swallowing the oncoming tide.

"Shame what happened to them," a man with more scars than teeth said kindly.

Ella looked over his shoulder to the troupe, their heads lowered in condolences as the bottle was passed between them all.

"Which one was it," the pin cushion haired woman asked.

"The ones who worship the spiked fella," someone said, more the inflection of a question on the last word than a statement.

"No, no," answered a short woman with a sharp nose, "It was the ones *who* spiked the fellas."

"That Fella?"

"No, any fellas. Or ladies. Just anyone who they think needs spikin'."

"Who *needs* spiking," the scarred man asked.

"It wasn't any of them," Ella interrupted. He took the extended bottle, tipped a pull of the bitter liquor, then said, "I had heard though."

"Well," said the man with the thick mustache as he took the bottle back, "Best you got away beforehand."

"Thank you," Ella said before turning to leave.

"Reason it's hard without a pack though," said someone behind him.

Ella turned to face the troupe and saw a large, orange lynx twelve hands high sat where the crate had been.

"I have-"

"-An empty church." The voice was lost in the crowd and liquor it had been too long since Ella had partaken in.

The man with a smile too big for his toothless grin

walked the lynx towards Ella. "But maybe you take our friend with you now. I know he'd love to see the mountains. It's where you're headed, yes?"

There was a warmth wrapped in disinterest on the lynx's face that softened Ella when the large beast ran his side against Ella's ribs. "Yeah, I think we are headed to the mountains."

III. THE PATH OF FAITH

Ella had yet to take the pilgrimage to the Haloed Ridge. Of course he had seen their silhouette smattered across the skyline – everyone had. All around the peaks were flat and flooded wetlands farmed by exiled witches who worked the irrigated rows that stretched on for miles atop stilts that kept their backward feet from spoiling the crops. Ella never questioned why blasphemers like witches were allowed to live, he only knew that when the brigades of Halos rode near, several veered off toward the mountain, often to never return.

Unlike the towns they had traveled through, no witches bowed or showed any sort of reverence to the Knights. They simply kept about their work, tools to the earth, brands upon their chests, only a few acknowledging the lynx who trailed behind Sir Crookedneck and Ella.

The three stayed to the front of the Haloed Order as none of the knights had spoken to Ella or Sir Crookedneck since the squire slayed the heretic. Instead, knights and their squires peeled off from the brigade until there was just the two of them and the lynx.

"Do you wish to bring the creature with you," Sir Crookneck asked.

"If you'll allow it."

Sir Crookedneck looked down from the mounted Elk Ella had fitted with bridle and saddle every morning since his indoctrination and said through a smile, "Your life starts anew today, Ella, I hope you take that with the weight it merits."

"What is happening today, sir?" He couldn't remember the last time he had called Sir Crookedneck, 'sir'. Maybe the fourth night, when the recognition of his new position finally outweighed the casual cadence he had developed in the circus. The squire did want to become a knight but what he had learned amongst them was they valued faith and action more than platitudes and pleasantries.

"Today," Sir Crookedneck said, pointing to the mountain path coming into focus, "we'll both be judged."

The path leading up the mountain was steep and winding. Switchback curves that sliced a narrow walkway flanked by a dropoff that increased in depth as they moved forward. Too thin for even children to walk shoulder to shoulder, they tied Sir Crookedneck's steed to a stone and began their march single file up the ridgeway. The knight insisted that he carry his own satchel and Ella understand the path they were each taking. The Lynx had been a shadow on a cloudy day to them. Often directly behind them, sometimes it veered off the steep embankment or into a thick brush or treeline only to reappear hours later – its lips wet and coat matted.

It was the smell of the peak Ella noticed first. The summer bin of a butcher shop when the wind picked up and blew rot and worms through your nose to fill your lungs. The lynx slithered through the loose rocks of the drop into a fog that Ella hoped was tinted purple by the sun.

"Is it much further," Ella asked.

Sir Crookedneck looked to his left where the thick fog rose and danced over his leather boots. "Not much longer at all now.

"First time I was here, I was no older than you. My

mother, she was a performer like you and your kin, she had worked tirelessly to get me engaged in the church. She was a sinner too. Someone I'd learn to call a wretch with my studies. The priests she sent me to realized I was more of the killin' kind, so they had me squire for the Haloed.

"When my liege brought me up this same path we're trekking now, I saw a light in his eyes like I'd never known."

Sir Crookedneck turned to face Ella and said, "I hope you see it in my own, Ella."

He was right. The knight's normal brown eyes were a glitter with specks of gold and green. An ocean of washing color that encased his onyx pupils. There was a sense of wonder Ella had never known to exist in those eyes, as if the knight was unsure and excited about that uncertainty for the first time in years. The squire felt like he could drown in them as his parents had done, the colour lapping over him until he just sank into the infinite.

Instead, he noticed the hand ahead of him.

It jutted from the mountainside with sharp and craggy angles. Fingers of weather worn rocks and appropriated dead tree limbs. The thumb was wider than the path they walked, with slightly thinner but longer mountain ledge fingers above casting shadows that spilled across the path. Within the mountain faced palm was a cave set on either side by firepits and priests.

Ella had never seen just the Holy of the Haloed before, his time having spent solely with their righteous fury. They were clothed in slim yellow pants that stopped between their knees and feet, their chests covered with a solitary halo of damp timber and another ring of light, that to the best of Ella's vision, emitted from nowhere but pure faith above their heads.

Sir Crookedneck acknowledged them with a solemn

nod, then bent his knee and faced Ella. "No matter what happens, those are holy folks. I'll fall, and you'll listen."

The Lynx stood behind Ella, its neck bent to cradle the crook of Ella's knee. "I don't understand." the boy said.

"You don't have to understand," the knight said. He stood, then marched down the path and toward the priests, "You just have to listen."

Much like the knights and witches along Ella's trek, the priests paid the squire no mind. Instead, they faced Sir Crookedneck and in one voice said, "Sir Davies Crookedneck, you wish to be judged in place of your squire at the Hand of God.

"Do you commit so? Your heart, your head, your halo, your neck?"

"Aye," the knight said with no hesitation.

"You may have your squire prepare you, then we agree to bear witness," the voice said. Ella realized even from his distance of fifteen yards that their mouths did not move and yet two voices spoke in unison and rang over the path like a bell.

"Ella, I'm ready for my last dress."

The squire remembered the mount left at the foot of the path and said, "But we didn't bring your armor."

Sir Crookedneck pulled the mail wrapped halo from his satchel, then said, "This is all I need."

Ella gently took the sharp circle of giant's bone and began to click it into the choker at the base of the knight's neck when Sir Crookedneck gently held the boy's wrist. "No," he said. "Not for battle, there's another notch at the front for judgment."

Ella had never seen Sir Crookednecks' neck clean shaven and therefore never noticed the small pin that jutted up just below his now hairless Adam's apple. In order to lock the halo into place, Ella understood the knight's head would have to be put through the circle. The squire's hands shook, the inner blade slicing the frayed edges of Sir Crookedneck's hair until it locked into place above his collarbone.

The knight stood, the glimmer in his eyes leaving a tail of glittered gold in the sharp mountain air when he turned.

Ella didn't understand why he felt so nervous until the Lynx said, "Even in uncertainty, he and all others of his ilk still walk."

The squire looked at the orange beast at his side. The Lynx's eyes were soft and thoughtful. Amongst the purple fog rising from the mountaintop and priests, the talking creature seemed as normal as the man who had been raising him walking along the suspended stone thumb of a God. "Reason it may be because of that uncertainty? That's what gives 'em faith." The lynx smiled and looked to Ella, "You and I know better though, yeah? Not so narcissistic as to think we can understand the incomprehensible. Them, though?" His large paw directed Ella's eyeline to Sir Crookedneck now at the tip of the Godthumb. The knight stood on his toes and threw a rope that had been tied to the back of the halo by the priests over the mountainous index finger. "They eat this shit up."

Ella suddenly understood – but before he could take a step, Sir Davies Crookedneck took his own. The halo the squire had sharpened so aptly made quick work of the knight's neck and spine. A faint hiss, a quick eruption of blood that sent a wave of red over the green canopy of branches, and the sound of wind rushing later, each part of the knight was gone to the fog that encased the mountain.

Their voice came again, "Sir Davies Crookedneck's heart has fallen to the right with his head to the left. In doing so, both he and you, Ella Flint, have been judged unworthy of The Lord's eternal love and therefore damned. You may collect his head to carry for the end of your days as penance. In Davies Crooked's sacrifice of heart, neither of you will be sent home. Ye shall both scatter the world eternally unloved and forsaken."

Without further explanation, the priests were gone. There was just Ella, the void of the knight's life, and the Lynx left. So when the orange beast began to scamper off the path and downhill toward the fog, the squire followed. He was careful to mind his footing, following the creature's every step on sure stone. The stench became so thick, Ella vomited onto the rocks. Then made sure to step over his bile to avoid slipping.

Then, the heads. The damned and rotted in various forms of decay. Hundreds of damned and forsaken heads that all veered left. The fog parted and Ella saw Sir Crookedneck's head atop the ramshackle hill of ghosts. The gold glimmer from his eyes gone, just a stare that bore through the young squire. He remembered it all, the lessons, fastening of armor, sharpening of halos, and standing ever at the ready for his liege.

Then, the voice. "Fuck 'em all."

Ella reeled back as the Knight's eyes flashed to purple.

Wisps of obsidian followed the severed head's irises when he said, "Give me a drop of your blood! I'll float the fuck out of here with an army of damned so pissed we'll slay every single one of those haloed shits. Unhinged bone and spite to burn their dog fucking deity to ash. We'll spit piss on the ashes of their Lord and vomit creatures this world hasn't had the grit to goddamn imagine. We'll raze their land and shit cities on the carcass of every God save ours, the one and true Lord Velmator!"

Ella had stepped back until he felt himself braced by the Lynx's soft fur. "Again," the Lynx said. "One god and fuck all others."

Ella turned to stare the Lynx dead in his soft green

eyes. "Maybe they're all wrong, kid. The ones who spike, get spiked – sever heads in faith, or wrap cities in tentacles."

The Lynx made a noise like a purr when he rubbed his head against Ella's hand. "Maybe it's just us. No gods to worship. Just our own vengeance to take and our own pack to answer to."

Ella remembered the tramps, the herbaceous liquor in his throat and soft smiles of the crowd. That's all he thought of when his boot crushed into the skull who was no longer the man who took him in.

Saved him.

IV. A BATTLEFIELD DEATH

Ella pulled a rotten branch from the mountainside and then unfurled the blood-soaked scarf from his hand. He pushed Sir Crookedneck's halo into the end of the long stick and wrapped the scarf – through the ring and around the branch – repeatedly until there was no scarf, halo, or branch left.

Just the weapon.

Ella carved his way up the mountain with no light or God in his heart.

Just the makeshift spear, hate, and the calm sensation of nothingness save himself.

KNIGHT RUMORS
OR THE FIVE PARTS
MATTHEW MITCHELL

I. THE BADGER KNIGHT

A Head

It is said that The Badger Knight lived here—right here in our town. My Sisters say The Badger Knight came to this place as a child, an orphan of the Bowling Wars. Our Father claimed The Badger Knight was born on a hill not far from us, and that he was there to witness the birth.

Jessa Mae's Father says much the same, but swears it was a hill closer to their own. Jessa Mae is my best friend, and she said that her Father knows best. She says that my Sisters and Father are fools.

I too believe The Badger Knight lived here, and that this is why The Badger Knight has returned. Why else would so great a Knight bear down on us in odious rage? This is a very small town after all, and there were so few of us to begin with. There must be a reason for the brutality, all this hurt.

Yes, I believe the Badger Knight was born in this town, and that it was a terrible, *awful* thing.

I wish I knew what caused The Badger Knight such agony in a lifetime before my own. Would that I could will away the pain brought to burden upon that pendulous, helmeted head…But I cannot.

No one seems to know why The Badger Knight has come for us, and if they do, they will have died with their dirty secrets before the sun dips beneath the bluff.

I hear screams coming down the hills.

There are no bird songs and the livestock have gone still. It is quiet until the screams, and when they start up again, it is jarring. Just an hour ago, I fear I may have heard Jessa Mae.

It has only been a day since The Badger Knight came to our town. A day in which so much has changed. There are not many stones left to turn; The Badger Knight has made great haste in rooting us from beneath every shadow. Sharp teeth behind the ebon helm snap and click. Almond shaped eyes burn in pools of yellow beyond the grated veil. Barks and growls echo in the hollow bascinet.

My Sisters say all hope is surely lost. They wail like necropolis maidens, and tell me we will be devoured soon. I am very afraid to die.

Despite our panic and our tears, we do not cast judgment on The Badger Knight, not I, nor my Sisters. Our Father was another story, but The Badger Knight took him, and so his former thoughts on such matters mean nothing. Not on Earth. In Hell, perhaps.

Whether or not these earthly offenses are punishable, I cannot say. It will not be our tender palms who extinguish the flame of The Badger Knight. How could we ever? The Badger Knight is great, and we are small. So very frail. Bare faced and soft headed.

We know not what this town means to The Badger Knight, and I will perish without discovery.

II. THE BEAN KNIGHT

A Heel

I HAVE HEARD that The Bean Knight wandered far from here before passing on from this world. A long, harrowing journey into the countryside which ended many lives. I do not know if there is truth to these claims, and will not be held accountable.

The Bean Knight was, of course, named so for wearing an armored coat composed of finely laced pellets that resembled soft legumes. When The Bean Knight walked, the beans clattered like bells, and all upon the road stayed away or came forward knowingly–knowing that they were to die.

It is said that each evening, as The Bean Knight slept beneath the stars, a terrible creature would soar through the sky before coming to roost upon the coat of iron beans. The Bean Knight awoke every morning with fewer beans quilted to the coat and their clattering grew more dim by the day.

The Bean Knight made less and less noise, and so more unexpected encounters ensued on the road. Innocents were slain, families torn apart, and children mashed like porridge. Chaos took root in the coiled soul of The Bean Knight, and new joys were found in murderous rampage.

As more iron beans disappeared from the coat, so too did its defensive capabilities. The Bean Knight suffered slashes and gouges. Digits were clipped, flesh was flayed.

Darkness flowed through the hardened veins of the Bean Knight, and an ancient pleasure was taken in pain.

Before long, death-ballads were written in the name of The Bean Knight; campfire stories sprouted in the wake of chiming iron beans. Warrants, bounties, and curses were cast with wild abandon on The Bean Knight's back. The people wanted blood, craved vengeance.

One evening as The Bean Knight slept upon a bed of bones, the abominable thiever of iron beans landed atop the dwindling coat. The Bean Knight—nearly nude save a small clutch of beans, bloody and ragged with wounds— awoke at once.

The story goes that The Bean Knight was beheld by a winged, mirror image. A slightly smaller, but no less fearsome clone. The only other visible difference between The Bean Knight and the visitor were the loathsome folded wings upon its back and the nearly-full coat of iron beans it wore.

"You are me," it said to The Bean Knight, "but I have wings, and now I will take all of your beans."

It is unclear why The Bean Knight gave up the remaining coat of beans to the winged visitor, but it was done without argument or bloodshed.

Morning saw The Bean Knight once more upon the road to wander aimlessly. Naked and bedraggled, the shadow of The Bean Knight soon filled with head hunters, thrill-seekers, and avengers of the dead. This must be where the story ends, for as we know, The Bean Knight did not return.

No, The Bean Knight never came home.

It has been said that there are chimes aloft the road at night, and great wings that rustle. Occasionally, one may also find an iron bean among the pebbles.

III. THE BAG KNIGHT

A Hand

I HAVE BEEN TOLD that when fog rolls in off the river—chill and blinding—The Bag Knight emerges from a black gutter. No one knows where the hole is, not for certain, but on dew blighted mornings the corpses of vagrants amass near the city walls. We are very blessed.

After a misty evening, some of us—the curious, the bold—will take an early stroll along the outer rim to survey the carnage. Some onlookers sit with pen and ink to sketch these grim scenes as intended works of art. To great applause, our city's most celebrated poet once gave a rousing performance while standing atop mounds of the freshly slaughtered. Other, less inspired individuals, will tussle and scrap to stake claim on the bodies in the name of science or the holy golden coin.

Many of us—the majority, I would think—simply dine with our eyes.

There is a sensational draw to these mass above-ground graves, a feeling of exhilaration and awe. We absorb the foul, fascinating energies within the proximity of victims made pocked and porous by a steel mace. I see God in what The Bag Knight creates with the arc of barbed chains and a ghoulish, serrated dirk.

It is a foul hobby, I will admit, and though I am deeply ashamed, I cannot look away.

There is talk of nasty weather tonight, and I ponder the horrors to be wrought on those who prowl and plunder the streets. Who among this rotting metropolis will meet their end by the tangled knot of a slick garotte? Perhaps the black toothed bully of West Street—that pocket picking derelict—will finally meet the razor's edge beneath the occulted glare of a murky moon. Will I recognize the faces of the dead on my morning pilgrimage—?

One can only hope.

To see a husk of life with which I am familiar is the sharpest of thrills. A religious experience. I can read milky spewage in the wastes of their sockets like tea leaves, and chart the sins by each lash. I decipher a ladder of evils leading to their demise, and fantasies of terror overtake me. Shrill visions of bonfire skewers through sizzling flesh. Desperate pleas for mercy beneath a pendulum swing. Ground meat and ichor ponds.

As I say, we are so very blessed.

When The Bag Knight brings cruel justice to this city, we feverish followers give thanks to the fog. We keep candles in our window, an earnest offerance, and ask that The Bag Knight grant us fresh vistas of ecstatic cosmosis. Hand to heart, we pray for the juggernaut birth— emerging from a drain, a void, a hole—and as heads fall to rest, we beg for blades flashing in the mist. There are dreams to be dreamt of the boiling river, and of lovely discoveries come dawn's first light.

I close my eyes and wonder if The Bag Knight knows my name.

IV. THE BANQUET KNIGHT

A Heart

When Father was a boy and Mother was his Queen, he would watch her from a window that faced the Tower of Pearl. Father often spoke of how it felt to see her rise above the spire in a gown of platinum, and that her dance through the sky made him very afraid. This was long before the Tower was taken by force and Mother had not yet returned to her people high above the world.

Father said he knew, even then, that The Banquet Knight would come for him. He assumed that his childhood days were running short and was anxious for it. Father understood that if he could see Mother, it meant that she was watching back.

Father was right, of course, and The Banquet Knight soon plucked him from the window. He said that the fate of his parents—my Grandmama and Grandpapa—were not known to him. Father's lineage was a topic of conversation that made him uncomfortable, and so I rarely inquired about the nature of my own.

After The Banquet Knight collected Father, he was then delivered to a brothel ship that floated off the coast. The brothel employed all manner of man and beast and its buffet of carnal professionals had been instructed to teach the stolen boy how to achieve great feats in his future marital chambers. It was well known that Mother, The Queen, did not sanction naivety in her chosen man-brides, and so Father had anticipated this outcome.

Father did not, however, expect The Banquet Knight to shield his innocence from the wet, squirming horde that inhabited the vessel. In every instance in which his virginity was made conquest, The Banquet Knight warded off the prostitutes with sickle and menace. In three years time, Father told me, he and The Banquet Knight disembarked the brothel ship with his purity undisturbed.

Two great falcons from the Tower of Pearl had been stabled at the wharf ahead of their arrival; Father and The Banquet Knight mounted the saddled birds and were flown to the University caverns over the course of several days. Once they arrived, Father was to be placed in the care of the blind, albinic professors who lectured in the caves. Father said Grandpapa once told him that each and every man-bride had been sent there to learn the secrets of death. Unlike the brothel ship, Father was eager to pleasure his mind and was not afraid of the depths to which the acquisition of knowledge would lead.

Similar to what had occurred in the waterlogged whore chambers of his youth, Father said The Banquet Knight did also resist any intended tutelage to be cast on him. The University staff—with their mirrored eyes and torches—insisted on Father's presence in the storied halls of stalagmite, but The Banquet Knight smote them and the pair rarely descended beyond the cavern mouth. Father's unrequited hunger to learn and be taught caused him great agony in those cold, dark years. Resentment grew behind his eyes.

When at last The Banquet Knight carried Father out of the University and into the light of day, a caravan of craftsmen greeted them upon emergence. The workers union was composed of skilled laborers from a diverse range of industries and they welcomed Father into their fold. The craftsmen informed him that Mother, Queen of all, insisted on his development as a contributing man-bride before the conclusion of betrothal. It seemed to Father that The Banquet Knight was wary of these intentions and thus he was not permitted to travel with the union en route to their encampment.

The Banquet Knight never slept, and so even though they had departed days after the laborers, Father was carried through the night and they soon passed the caravan. It was a lonely pilgrimage from then on and the pair crossed many borders. In absence of the ornery, chattering union men he had briefly met, Father discovered that he craved their company.

Father told me that when they arrived at the encampment, he was met with a dizzying array of workshops that smoked and churned beneath the shadow of an enormous, volcanic forge. Men of every nation toiled happily there. Father said their comradery and strength cowed him to tears. He was eager to use his soft hands, to harden them with fire and triumph, but once they had settled into their quarters, The Banquet Knight barred the door. Father was further denied the thrilling, exacerbating work he was promised and it pained him. It seemed strange, he told me, that all he had been taught to anticipate as a boy had now passed him by.

One day, not long after Father had grown his beard, The Banquet Knight took him by the hand. The Banquet Knight produced a satchel of silk ribbon and braided his beard in the matrimonial style. Father said The Banquet Knight trembled through the weaving and that tears clanged inside the helm like raindrops on hot roofing. When he was braided and beautiful, Father was led out of the union encampment and the two journeyed back to the Tower of Pearl.

Mother took Father as her man-bride before her court of prostitutes, professors, and professionals. They watched the ceremony with tight lips and hooded eyes. As was custom, Mother had removed herself from the royal seat—an act otherwise unpermitted in the glory of day. While she danced the courtship-waltz, The Banquet Knight occupied the throne in her stead. The court would not cast eyes upon The Banquet Knight and they crossed their arms in distaste.

Mother, the Queen, ended the courtship-waltz with a kiss upon Father's hip. He told me his skin burned at the touch of her lips and that his groin morphed into something hard and unexpected. Father emitted the man-bride seed upon the Tower floors and the court of prostitutes exploded in anger.

The whores and whorebeasts pointed out Father's moist mistake and aired their grievances. They told their

Queen that Father had not learned of himself and that The Banquet Knight was to blame. Mother slew the Captain of the brothel ship to silence this outcry and the head rolled to Father's feet.

Father said he had never seen blood so abundant that it pooled in shades of purple and he expelled the contents of his stomach right there upon the puddle of seed. The Queen's court of pale professors scratched at their shaded bifocals. They shrieked and gave an affluent, impassioned rebuke on The Banquet Knight's dismissal of their tutelage; proclaimed that Father, her current man-bride, would not have buckled beneath the weight of death had they been allowed to teach him.

Mother then demanded that Father remove the decapitated head from the Tower floor. Father told me he bent at the waist to oblige, but that the head was too heavy and he could not lift it. His smooth fingers gained no purchase on the blood-slicked flesh. His thin muscles bore no flex. His pores clogged with unfamiliar sweat. Father nearly fainted and collapsed into his sticky purgings.

The court of union workers rattled their tools and stomped their dusty boots. They cursed The Banquet Knight for producing such weakness in Father and stated that had they been afforded his apprenticeship, Mother, their Queen, would surely be wedded to a man-bride of fortitude and skill.

In his prone state, Father said that Mother dipped down beside him and bunched her gown up to her knees. He watched as she scooped his fallen fluids into her claws and pushed the mess between her thighs. Father could not be sure, as he was still dazed, but believed he saw me swell in her belly within moments of the act.

The Banquet Knight, as we all know, then rose from Mother's throne and expressed a deep love for Father, her man-bride. It was then that Father noticed tear drops rusted the helm, and he understood that The Banquet Knight had wept for many years in his company. The Banquet Knight commanded Mother to release Father and divorce him in the name of their blazing passion.

The court went silent and so too did Mother, for The Banquet Knight had always served one purpose and never faltered. Father spoke at last from where he lay on the floor. He told The Banquet Knight that he did not share this love and that, in fact, he blamed The Banquet Knight for forsaking him the life he was promised.

In light of Father's dismissal, the taking of the Tower began and The Banquet Knight made short work of Mother's court. Before Father's very eyes, the throne was also destroyed and soon, he knew, both he and his Queen would follow.

Mother, in her endless wisdom, took Father in her claws by the flesh of his back and flew away to her home in the sky. It was there that I was born and it is from above that I watch. For many years, I saw little below but heard much from Father, and as my eyes have grown stronger, I begin to see the world as Mother once did.

From on high, I have often watched The Banquet Knight wander alone in the Tower of Pearl, and though there are no windows here, I fear one day I will be seen— plucked from the sky and taken away.

V. THE BLOOM KNIGHT

A Hole

I TAKE lives for my own amusement. It brings me such joy. I do not go to slaughter with false notions of honor dulling my brutality; the carnage I produce with blade or bow or finger is butchery, pure and unbridled. Dealing pain is pleasure and I hope to die screaming in the faces of those I sought to vanquish.

What should I tell you of my history? There is much to know and I wonder what is most important. How to best use these few moments we have together, that is always the question.

Here is what I will say:

I slipped from a moist crevice of stars and fell to earth —feet first—with a blight upon the flesh. From nose to breast, a lavender storm encompasses my body. It is hard like a callous and rich with varying hues, as you see. The bruise does not hurt, but in this life that means so very little.

I am not shunned for my flowering rash, however, and have often been called beautiful by those who picked the wrong receiver of advances. Rather, I am discounted because of my nature and, despite the allure of my physical form, a terror lurks beneath.

The Goddesses marked me a monster, or so I have been told. Your people say my blight is a warning to those who would seek to reach me in lust or drunken fever. *Do Not Touch*, flashing in purple flesh, *Stay Away*.

Marked for sport, I have always presumed. Given a lovely bruise and a brain with gnashing teeth by deities in need of a jester. Targeted in some grand comedy to entertain heavenly bodies who would be better served granting mercy on the wretches who fail to cross the road when I pass.

Shit upon the divine: that is what I believe. *Fuck them all. And fuck you too.*

Have you heard of my axe? I beg you to call it by its name—the name your people gave it. Do you know from where my axe was claimed—?

There is a bog beneath glacial boulders to the North, and only I had the strength to unearth it. I am terribly strong, as you must also surely see. There, in the briny swamp, I pulled my axe from the skull of an undead King…

No, that is incorrect. I have misspoken. The bog is where I found the sword. The axe, the axe, the axe… Where did I—?

Oh, yes! How ridiculous of me. Of course I remember: the Pond of Null, beyond the darkest grove. I reached down into the mercury waters and hauled it from a sunken battlefield; wrenched it free from the hands of a drowned God who forged it. My axe is very special, and I know you know its name.

What else should one know about me before the end? I often wonder how it feels to hear these last words. What would *I* inquire of *my* destroyer—?

Nothing, I suppose. But that is me, and you are you. Never forget that. We are not alike, not kin, different breeds.

I am The Bloom Knight and you are my quarry.

NEVER THREATEN A SPIDER
SARA CENTURY

THE BLADE AGAINST VIY'S RIBS SLIPPED AND BROKE SKIN, sprouting a thin stream of blood. Far below her, the gray bog gurgled like a hungry belly. The three silver-clad women, Viy's would-be captors, held their knives out at her. Beneath the drop-off, the bodies of lost travelers jutted out at odd angles, each at a different stage of decomposition. Even from high above, the stench was dizzying.

Viy kept her eyes trained between the women, hoping she might still talk her way out of this. "I'm just passing through," she lied, holding her hands up in mock surrender.

"We *know* who you are," said the first among them. Like her sisters, she held a long, thin knife in either hand and wore shimmering silver chainmail that sparkled too brightly in the dreary light of the bog. Younger than the other two, her light pink skin did not crease as she frowned at Viy. At her feet was Viy's backpack and sword, which they'd taken after catching her by surprise as she attempted to cross this vile passage. Viy looked feral by comparison to the three; nearly naked and covered in sweat and mud. Her eyebrows were thin and her eyes a pale blue, coolly reflecting Viy's desperate expression. "We know why you've come."

"They can't have valued you much if they sent you here," said the second, the eldest of the three but still no older than thirty. A mocking, incredulous smile tugged at the edge of her lips. Her dark brown eyes bounced between Viy and her sisters, eyebrows heavy as two charcoal marks. "It's called Dead Man's Bog for a reason, you know."

"I'm not here to -" Viy began, but she silenced herself when the blade pushed just a bit deeper into her flesh. The stream of blood at her side widened, and unwelcome tears welled in her eyes.

"Don't you think it's so undignified to lie?" wondered the third, bemusedly looking into Viy's eyes while pressing against the knife's handle. Her olive skin was dotted with dark brown freckles, and her green eyes glittered in the faint light of the sun. "You'll have to come with us to meet the queen, now."

Viy started to speak, but the words weren't there. The truth of why she'd come to the wetlands was tangled, but there was no denying that these women were right about her. She'd come here to steal from them; a job handed down from the very King who had exiled her. Just to get this far, she'd undertaken fourteen miserable days of travel, each minute only driving home what a mistake it all was. Damp days, full of soggy bread and water-logged boots, dodging nests of snakes, devoured by insects…worst of all, wondering what she was doing any of it *for*.

Capture would lead only to torture and death, and was not an option. She'd rather die in this miserable place than go with them. The cliff's edge called to her. It meant nothing but the sliver of a chance, but she had little left to lose. She checked the women's faces one last time for any hint of compromise, but there was none. Summoning the last reserve of energy in her travel weary body, she shoved away from them. A shriek escaped her as the knife in her side slipped free, and she leapt from the drop-off, crashing down the bank into the shallow pool. Unseen to her, three sets of eyes watched as she crashed into the water's mossy surface. Soon, they vanished into the haze, as if they'd never been there at all.

DEAD MAN'S Bog was home to an enormous cave system, its scope unfathomable to outsiders. To survive this treacherous stretch of land was a rarity; many a war had been lost by armies attempting to cross it. A well-worn road had been established around the bog that allowed travelers to completely avoid it. Yet, as with any hazardous zone, there were countless tales of what treasures might lie within for anyone brave enough to seek them out.

Legend has it that, at the heart of these caves was a great cavern, located ambiguously "near the swamp's center." This was said to be the final resting place of a forgotten queen, who ruled her people with an iron fist. Tall tales spoken by rugged travelers established that her tomb was the home of a powerful jewel, protected by the long-dead matriarch's unknown and unnamed descendants.

It was rare that anyone ventured as deep into their realm as Viy had, but she had come in King Atticus's name to find this gem. According to him, it would grant the city of Antioch protection from the plague, if paired with the right combination of spells from the mages. This was not the first such job he'd given her; after all, she had gained notoriety only the year before when she stole the Golden Eye of the Cosmic Newt from Bernard of South Arcadia.

When other mercenaries had marveled that the task was surely impossible, Viy was known to retort, "Maybe for *you*." Yet, she'd quickly come to regret her swagger, as it only led to increasingly dangerous missions from the king.

Even knowing that she had no real choice in the matter, she'd taken the job grudgingly. Whatever her flaws, far-flung flights of fancy weren't generally among them. If she were to risk her life, she'd rather it be for reasons more substantial than a myth. Yet, King Atticus was the only one who could end her exile, and so she did as he asked.

The pool Viy had fallen into was in a treacherous spot, with a steep, eroding drop-off on one side, and on the other, a bank full of sinkholes, with no firm ground to stand on. Horses, humans, and giant cats had been caught here, their bodies now either skeletal or badly decomposed. Flesh drifted from their bones in globs, no longer resembling its prior form.

Despite it all, the bog was not a place of death, but of life. The heavy mist that made it untenable for human travel created a perfect climate for frogs, turtles, snakes, and more. Even this desolate graveyard, filled with lost souls, was the home of countless insects and birds. Each nameless corpse contributed to a thriving ecosystem. Though they had each come here to hunt for food or treasure, they had instead given the ultimate gift in death.

Viy vaguely registered that she was in danger, but her desire to sleep was so strong that it no longer mattered. In her hazy state, she imagined herself back home in Antioch. She was with Aelia once more, and the putrid pond water she was sinking into was a warm, bubbly bath. She drifted through her memories like a ghost, viewing prior days of happiness as an impartial witness. Aelia, kissing her forehead. "Nothing will change my love for you," she'd said. Now, torn and tattered by years of hard travel and haunted by her work as a thief and killer for the King, Viy wondered if that were still true. If it had ever been true…

Still, even as tired as she was, something, some horrible noise, wouldn't let her sleep. A distant but persistent thumping sound. It reminded her of something. She couldn't place it. She didn't want to open her eyes to see. She'd been dreaming about something. What was it? The sound had ruined it. Something lovely and forgotten. The thumping got louder.

Viy was angry when she opened her eyes. It took seconds to identify the sound. Up on the edge of the drop-off, amid the gnarled trees of the forest, there stood a small black and silver rabbit. It stared at her wild-eyed, stamping its feet. Despite herself, her anger dissolved. She chuckled, but it came out as a violent cough. "Stupid rabbit," she rasped.

Now awake, Viy was forced to register the horror of her surroundings. She thrashed suddenly, her body instinctively recoiling from its environment. The smell of death was unbearable, and hungry birds eyed her from above. The wound in her side throbbed, begging to be cleaned and cared for. Her aching bones screamed at her to give up, but the sensation of swamp slime against her skin was far too revolting to rest in. She had no choice but to try and survive, if only to die in a less offensive place.

She struggled to stand, but the quagmire was not a standing place. She barely managed to get upright, splashing and wading through the muck as best she could. The tangled roots of fallen trees and the bones of the fortunate dead scraped against her as she moved, threatening to pull her under. More than once, she froze, certain that one of the bodies drifting alongside her had moved under its own power. Her vision blurred with mud, it was impossible to tell for sure. But she could hear movement that was not her own, and the thought of what it might be chilled her.

After an eternity, Viy heaved herself onto a crumbling ledge. She warbled like an injured bird, stammering a few incoherent words of triumph between gasps for air. Seemingly of their own accord, her hands grabbed at leaves, trying desperately to wipe the gore from her stab wound. With assorted flora plastered to her side, she finally dared to look back down at the water's edge. From her relative place of safety, she stared in disbelief as the dead twitched and stirred, drifting in unison toward her. A fallen cat's claws, barely attached to its rotting legs, swiped wildly in her direction. A dead bird screamed from a broken beak. Human skeletons, still clad in the heavy armor that sank them, shambled toward the ledge. A strange, collective moaning filled the air, and Viy knew that she had to move.

In her battered state, it might have been hours or days that it took to reach the spot she'd jumped from. More than once, the earth simply collapsed out from under her, sending her sliding perilously back toward the waiting arms of the dead. No longer caring about survival, her goal became only to fight the eroding hill so ferociously that it, and the rest of this damned swamp, would always remember her.

Eventually, Viy clawed her way back to the top of the slope and collapsed in the grass. She retched water from her lungs, the cut in her side screaming so fiercely that it brought her to her knees. Unable to move any further, she wondered if it wouldn't have been easier to simply let the corpses rip her to shreds.

The rabbit sat patiently as if it had been waiting for her. No longer thumping its feet, it seemed puzzled by the wretch that had fallen before it. Viy glared, her breath coming in great gasps. She felt an irrational anger toward this creature for daring to urge her to save her own life. Neither of them moved for a long time.

The rabbit twitched nervously. Viy noticed then that it was dangerously underfed, with a slight injury to its neck, likely from the tooth of a predator that had only just missed its mark. This was no swamp rabbit; indeed, it didn't look like a wild rabbit, at all. She puzzled at how it might have come to be here, only just realizing that the stomping was its way of asking for her help.

"Those creepy monsters scared you, huh?" she said finally, her gaze softening. "No, *I* wasn't scared. I can see why *you* were, though."

Viy wondered if she should continue her quest. She desperately wished to see what remained of her family, and Aelia…Aelia, who she had loved, before fate had torn them apart. The promise of these things had kept her going for so long, but the harder she tried, the more distant they seemed. Even if she succeeded, there was no guarantee that Atticus would end her exile. She sighed. More likely, she would die out here, twisted into something unrecognizable to her loved ones, never to see any of them again.

Amid her soul-searching, the rabbit had crept up to Viy's side, lowering its head to her. Gently, she patted its ears. "I won't let them get you," she said, or tried to say. Her voice was raw and useless, and she decided to let it rest. Hidden in a patch of leaves under a dead tree, she and the rabbit slept.

THE DAY WAS dim and clouded. Uncertain of how much time had passed since she collapsed in fitful slumber, Viy decided that there was little choice but to travel on. A soft, pleasant humming sound floated through the trees, and, without understanding why, she chose to follow it. She began walking, and the rabbit hopped dutifully along behind her.

Viy's bag of tools were long gone, and she hardly knew where they were heading. She had only a fallen branch to use as a club, if need be, and a comically unconcerned rabbit at her side. Finding a single jewel in the sprawling swamp, regardless of the unique power it was said to hold, was a ludicrous proposition. As the days passed, it grew more likely that she would simply wander the woods feeding on bugs until she died. Still, the hum was intoxicating, and she and the rabbit drifted toward it.

When she'd all but given up hope she'd ever find the mythical cave, she saw the women once more. They stood casually at the entrance, talking amongst themselves. Viy realized that this was her destination, and pulled the rabbit back, hiding it in a brush pile.

"If I tell you I'll come back, that means I have to live through this, or I'm a liar, right?" she smiled. "I'll see you soon." The rabbit did not seem to appreciate the weight of this statement, and nervously chewed on a nearby twig as Viy walked away.

With her companion now relatively safe, Viy ran up on the women in a fury, club in hand. The still biting knife wound in her side demanded that their blood be spilled in turn. She struck at them with lightning speed, bones cracking beneath her blows. With two quickly disarmed and the youngest woman shoved to the ground, Viy raised the club over her head, ready to crush her skull if need be. Instead of fighting back, the woman stared back with no expression at all, as if nothing had happened. "Where's the jewel?" Viy shouted, but to no avail. As the seconds passed, the woman ceased to be, fading into the mist.

Viy staggered backwards, unable to grasp what she had

seen. The other two women vanished after their sister, leaving no trace of themselves behind. The club fell uselessly from her hands. "What is this?" she asked aloud. Baffled, her attention was soon diverted again by the hum. She turned to search for its source.

The jewel! Even tucked deep in the dark tunnels ahead, it glowed like a beacon. But not just that. It was singing. A low, beautiful song, drifting through the bramble, in harmony with the forest around it. This was the sound that had guided her here, now so much louder. The gem radiated an energy that was pleasing to all her senses, lulling her into a state of calm as it bathed the inside of the cave with yellow and purple light.

In the presence of the gem, Viy felt deep contentment. She was no longer concerned with the king, the quest, or the vanishing women. Even Aelia and Antioch faded from her mind. She only wanted to be closer to the jewel. And, she thought absently, to see the rabbit safe. No! Better than safe. This rabbit would be a ruler among rabbits, adorned with priceless jewelry and silk robes, sitting beside Viy on the sparkling throne of the long-dead queen.

At the entrance of the cave, a transparently pale but beautiful woman walked toward her, perhaps sixty or seventy years of age, wearing a dark purple robe. Her white hair was pulled back from her face, and her neck and wrists were adorned with heavy gold jewelry. She held both hands out to Viy.

"You've finally come!" she said merrily. "My girls were meant to bring you days ago. But you've finally come!"

Viy's feet seemed to move on their own. There was something hypnotic in the woman's gaze, compelling her to approach. "You sent them?" she asked, her words slurring. "Why?"

"I am the queen you seek," the woman explained, her voice brimming with kindness. "You need not struggle any longer. You came for the jewel? My daughter, I have treasures beyond your imagining! You may have it!"

Viy looked around, not fully registering anything she was seeing. The more she tried to make out the forest that surrounded them, the brighter the light grew, until it was nearly blinding her. "Oh. Are you sure?"

"Of course, girl. I understand you completely," the queen assured her. The light changed suddenly, and she was engulfed in shadow. Her voice remained bright and pleasant, but the hint of a rasp now tinged its edges. "Thanks to my kindness, you no longer need to return to the king, or your old city. My throne has been empty for so long, but *you* are meant to rule in my place. The jewel, the throne, it's yours for the taking, dear. Go!"

"If you're sure you don't need it," Viy murmured pleasantly, forgetting that she'd been ready to bludgeon a stranger to death only moments before. Unable to see the sudden hint of malice in the queen's eyes, she took slow, uncertain steps toward the - jewel? Throne? Treasure? She could no longer quite tell what awaited her at the end of the tunnel.

But what was that noise? Quick, loud thumps. She shook her head with displeasure at the interruption, glancing back. The rabbit stood against the darkness of the forest, illuminated by the light of the moon. It stood, alert, and stamped its feet emphatically. Viy turned back to the queen, whose smile had faded into a sneer. As the others had vanished before, she began to fade from Viy's sight. Behind her, or perhaps within her, there appeared a shadow, small at first but growing rapidly. Where once the woman stood, there was now only the form of a great spider, so large that its shadow filled the cave's entrance. Viy stared blankly into a reflection of her own worried, dirt-streaked face, recoiling as she realized she was looking into one of the spider's many eyes.

With the slight movement of its enormous head, the spider's fangs came into view, dripping cloudy pools of venom onto the cave floor. Her web sparkled all around her, radiating with the ethereal light that Viy had once mistaken for treasure. With a shudder, Viy reversed course, falling back into the dirt as the spider's ticking, echoing laugh rose through the air. In place of the jewel was, in fact, a glowing white egg sac, hidden deep within the cave. Hundreds of oversized baby spiders writhed beneath its surface, fighting for release. As Viy looked on in horror, a single leg pierced its gauzy prison, and dozens of newborns ripped their way to life.

Viy staggered to her feet, realizing that it had all been a trick. There was no jewel, no treasure, no silver-clad women, no crawling corpses. The queen, if ever she had existed to begin with, was long dead. There was only the spider god, singing its haunting song to lost travelers, luring them closer to her cave so that she and her children might feed.

Filled with an unexpected desire to survive, Viy snatched up the rabbit in both arms and rushed through the trees. Like a deer pursued by a pack of wolves, she darted and dodged through the brush. Tumbling down ravines, splashing through streams, losing direction time and again, she held the frightened rabbit for dear life.

For days, they fled the spiders, stopping only to nap or scrounge for food. All the while, the spider god's laughter rang through her skull. Night after night, illusions haunted her. Several times over, she found herself being called into danger by some flickering vision of the past. Ghostly images of her sister, her grandmother, Aelia, and others she'd known, beckoning her to walk off a cliff's ledge or into the jaws of a waiting alligator. In each case, the rabbit's insistent stomp brought her to her senses just in time.

The spider's reach was long, but it was not infinite. As the thick swamp became a thinning marsh and the danger slowly began to ease, she finally gave the rabbit a name. "You are Jewel," she said aloud, finally able to laugh without pain. "I was sent to find a jewel and I did."

Viy had no plan for what she and Jewel would do once they left the wetlands. To explain this improbable story to the king meant she would be deemed not just an exile, but a coward and a fool, besides. Part of her burned at the thought, but nothing - no quest, no king, and no hidden longing for what might have been - *nothing* could force her to return to the swamp of the spider god and her hungry, roaming children.

QUEEN OF THE FIRE ARCH
CHARLES AUSTIN MUIR

May we burn bright like the Dawn Gates
  And seize our destiny with indomitable heart,
  While others judge us reckless who know not
  Where we came from,
  Nor whither we go.

— "INVOCATION TO KEVASTRA"

~As transcribed for Queen Regent Derenna on the eve of the Second Cabal War~

My name is Danak. I can tell none of you recognize me. This is not surprising, as I held a minor position in the Royal Court. And yes, that is our flag waving behind me in the sea breeze; I'm sailing the *Champion* by means of the Queen's sigils. Expect me to reach the shore within three days... alone. Let me repeat that: *Alone.*

As of now, Derenna, *you* shall rule as Regent. The sooner we install your daughter, the better. But we can discuss that in the coming days.

I realize too well the enormity of my words. But you must listen. The majority of you take me for some sort of trick... perhaps by one of Panog's allies. *Yet I swear to you that I serve the Fire Arch.* Before I joined this expedition, I was a teacher of philosophy and healing, a fact that you can easily verify. More importantly, in secret, I assisted the Queen in a manner more intimate than anyone can ever know.

Not that I can prove it... though how else do you suppose I would know about the Black Pool? Who else but its sole master could empower me to speak to you through it? But there are too many of you gawking at me, emanating fear and suspicion. Unless you serve on the War Council, you must leave the Vault of Mirrors. And tell no one what you have witnessed here; behave as if Queen Kevastra is coming home.

As for the rest of you... when I arrive, we cannot afford to belabor what has passed. Therefore, through the oculus of the Black Pool, I will give you a full account of events on Mount Verashus so we may form plans as soon as I rejoin you. Furthermore, you must understand that we shall have neither mourning period nor burial rites, for we have no time and nothing to bury. Not all is grim, however: Panog serves our Queen now, his spirit confined to the Taming Yoke of Eternity.

And while we have lost Kevastra to the Realms Between, she continues to watch over us. Perhaps one day, from the loins of a slave child much like her mother, she will return to us.

Most of you silently refuse to consider a single word I've said. How could a sorcerer as powerful as the Queen fall to a minor magician? But the truth is she suffered far worse from her victory over the Crucible House than she made known to anyone. During her battle with the Six Lords, Panog snuck a poisonous braid into her hair that penetrated her brain and wove into her nerves like a thin, boiling vine—not potent enough to kill her on the spot, but enough to corrode certain vital functions over time.

As a result, she fell gravely ill after destroying Panog's cohorts... themselves betrayed by him when he abandoned the fight to nurse his wounds. So it is that an inferior sorcerer not only escaped our leader, but mortally wounded Kevastra...

Hold your tongues! I tell you Panog managed the inconceivable! Not through some special breakthrough on his part, but through the spell-work of his betters. Think about it: Although six mages could not defeat her, in the end their combined attack exhausted her defenses against certain noxious forces, earthly or otherwise. So that, recognizing the need for secrecy when she came back, she hid herself from even her closest companions, to combat the venom under nearly the same fragile conditions that you or I would.

And this is where I entered directly into her service... through the dreaming gateway she adjured me to assist her, for although we had never met, she had read my treatise on curing afflictions with Thargic Stones.

ON THE FIRST of seven days, I carried out Kevastra's instructions for drawing out the poison. Her bedchamber became an armory of healing stones, runes, and sigils. Among the gatekeepers she had me summon was Ral-Bazure, the Shadow Demon, who, though insufferable by nature, gave her spirit refuge from the agonies raging through her ravaged body. On the third day, the Thargic Stones raised her condition to the peak of crisis. Mind you, be grateful she instructed me to protect you all with a binding spell throughout this ordeal; for I will never be haunted by a ghost so cruel as the memory of what I witnessed during that time.

Of her torments in her sickbed, I will say only that her eyes took on a frightful, grassy color, as of spoiled milk; and that the fluids weeping through her skin gave off a sour odor so pungent that I feared you would smell it wafting from her suite, penetrating even the binding spell.

I admit I was not in a sound state of mind as the slimy poison continued to exude from her. My hands began to itch from a devilish heat and my insides seethed as if they had caught fire. The symptoms only intensified as her body deteriorated into a deathlike state that looked impossible to overcome. On the fifth night, the very moribund sight of our mighty Queen, soiled and shriveled beyond recognition, finally dropped me to my knees in a paroxysm of sobbing.

But it was then that I glimpsed an opening in the dark wood of her struggle! For with startling vigor, her slick hand seized mine and her voice uttered inside my head:

"*We will get through this.*"

As she spoke, a giddy feeling spread through me as if I had eaten some intoxicating plant. A living warmth feathered beneath my skin like ribbons of glittering light infused with all the colors of sunrise on clear water. Past, present, and future undulated through these glowing caresses from within, and I felt myself dissolving into the loving arms of immortality.

For what seemed like both a moment and eternity, I wondered what we had to get through; then the energy flowed away from me like a gift that was not meant to be owned yet, and I found myself at the Queen's bedside once more.

Thus forced back into duty, I gave no more thought to the vastness that had embraced me, for the feeling of its absence made my limbs heavy... a mocking encumbrance.

My only relief was that my symptoms had disappeared, although I had begun to think of them as part of my vigil.

Two days later, Kevastra's eyes opened; they were hers again.

"You're back," I cried, and in my amazement, kissed our kingdom's founder on the cheek.

"For now. Panog's poison is stable, but only for a time. I've lost too much strength to eradicate it. The venom continues to work on my brain... we've slowed its progress, but eventually it will increase."

"How long will that take?"

Her voice grew flat and distant. "Long enough for me to take advantage of it when I part Panog's head from his bony little body."

Well, as you recall, when she convened the War Council the next morning, she looked pallid and gaunt, not surprising for someone who had dispatched five of the world's greatest sorcerers singlehandedly. Yet, by casting another binding spell upon the court, she tricked you all into perceiving her at full strength, so that no one could weaken her faith in her abilities or throw the kingdom into a panic.

Such, also—if you haven't guessed—was her reasoning for concealing her attempt to overcome the venom that had become part of her.

And that is why the news I bear sends a jolt through each of you that defies all sense; you were shielded from any doubts that Kevastra would return in good health with Panog's head chained inside an iron coffer.

AT THIS POINT you are wondering how I took part in the raid on the sorcerer's temple. The truth is, although I refused to think of her dire self-prediction, a part of me panicked at the idea of us separating—as though I, and not she, were the orphaned child—and so I begged the Queen to let me accompany her warriors. With considerable reluctance she consented to my proposal, admitting that I had demonstrated abilities suitable enough for her purpose.

The night before we set sail, we held a secret meeting with the crew, who alone knew of her condition. Assembled on the bow, we sealed a blood compact over the sigil of the Fire Arch, each of us aware that our odds had changed with the Queen battling poison in her brain. By dawn, we were underway, many of you watching us as Kevastra went to battle on this plane for the last time.

As I mentioned, Panog serves the Queen now in the Realms Between. Unfortunately, I cannot provide physical evidence of this, for I left what remains of their bodies on Mount Verashus. I can, however, assure you that I am proof not only that Kevastra broke the Crucible House, *but that she fell in battle in such a way that a part of her lives on in me.* And mark you, for I know this sounds blasphemous... I swear to you I will prove it! But until that time, prepare yourselves for the certainty that I alone, a teacher you have never heard of, shall disembark from the *Champion* once she is moored.

There: The secrets, the deceptions, have been revealed. Most of you still refuse to believe me... yet you are beginning to see an unsettling cohesion in what I say. The picture rings true with certain notions many of you have had about our Queen, but have never dared to make public. Even as your skepticism persists, you are pricked by pangs of betrayal; this makes you question your profoundest beliefs about our ruler.

But let me ask you this: Would some of you feel so misled if a king, instead of a queen, had sat on the throne?

Remember that the qualities that offend you now are the ones that united the tribes and established a kingdom! As the Scrolls point out, no government in our people's history has ascended from a sovereign so ambitious and fierce... an abused orphan who slaughtered her mother's killers and overthrew a tyrant *by the age of nine.* We are the beneficiaries of Kevastra's reinvention under conditions rarely encountered on the road of kings.

And be honest with yourselves: She spared you a truth you did not want to see. Again, be glad you did not witness what I did in her bedchamber.

Of course, my body and social status make it easy for me to speak this way. I raise these points because the shock of her death threatens to cloud your judgment. Like Kevastra, we must crush all doubts for the Fire Arch to survive and grow strong again; perhaps it will help you to know what she told me on the voyage:

"Most of my advisors could not understand why I insisted on taking on the Six Lords all at once and by myself. They accused me of being selfish and reckless, although they expressed their objections in milder terms. In their defense, I could not explain to them what it meant to me to show our enemies that a cabal like the Crucible House could be broken by one woman. Whatever happens, whatever people tell you, just know that I needed to do everything the way I did it. There is a plan at work that escapes even me; but in the end, all will be known."

She was right, as you will see. At the time though, I gave little thought to what her promise might mean... for the towering outline of our destination soon shuddered into view.

JUDGING by the sudden chill and darkening skies, our adversary had been waiting for us. Unlike her expedition to the Crucible House—when she rendered herself invisible to the Eye of the Six Lords—Kevastra had conserved her powers at sea, thereby exposing our approach to those who would scry on us. Within moments the moderate winds had freshened into a gale and the sea increased to a heavy swell, engulfing us in a wilderness of foaming rollers.

All this was to be expected, for she had warned us that Panog could exert an elemental influence with limited reach; not that this allayed our anxiety as we stroked the oars amidst the onslaught.

Soon the waves grew higher, their crests breaking into the spindrift and hurling spray on us like spongy serpents conjured from the seawater. Yet the ship's wallowing lessened as the Queen cast a maneuvering spell to help us maintain speed against the fury of the squalls and black, foaming hills that tumbled and spat on us.

It began to seem as if we might reach the beach with no further opposition; but then Kevastra broke into our thoughts with a stern command, "*Shields*," for her voice would have been drowned in the roaring gale; at which point the rolling panorama gave way to an all-encompassing shroud of dingy yellow ice crystals. Owing to its appearance and odor of decay, I would not call this phenomenon a fog.

Shields gripped tight, we peered into the heavy veil. A premonition crept into us arising from the blind sensation of the seas suddenly easing up, releasing us in perfect synchrony with the noxious cloud washing over the ship and piercing our senses with its stench. Soon we were sealed even from each other, as we sat statue-still searching the thickness of ice crystals for signs of hostility.

Then, a frenzied succession of splashing sounds as several attackers sprang from the waters and flung themselves onto the ship; the weight of the veil took on a dreamy coherence set off by the motions of ghostly silhouettes clambering over the gunwales.

The cloud began to stir up as the creatures threw themselves upon the roof of our upraised shields. We were able to thrust them back into the sea at first, but they quickly overtook us, piling over each other and pummeling our defense as they boarded us in growing number. Seated at the oars, we could do little but beat at them with our swords—those nimble enough to draw them in the tumult —and fend off their blows until they had begun to split our shields.

Several times we nearly capsized as we fought them off in this clumsy fashion, unable to make out anything but portions of the dripping, scraggly shapes looming over us like vengeful apparitions in the swirling chaos.

With my own eyes I had observed only the swipes of large, taloned hands, until one of the creatures broke my shield and thrust its face into mine with its warm, putrid breath brushing my cheek. Its features resembled those of a bat, yet bore the stamp of a cruel, almost human intelligence. It would have taken its time with me, for it seemed to savor my despair like the scent of a luscious fruit it had traveled far to devour.

But then Kevastra's voice boomed from a distance well above her place next to me; her words sounded like no tongue I had ever encountered, and within moments the eddying veil began to dissipate, taking the bat-like monsters with it.

Impressions flooded over us then as swiftly as our vanished attackers. Mount Verashus rearing into the sky; sunbeams lancing through a cloud break; the tang of the sea air; low swells and mild breezes; the empty processes of a dull gray afternoon. We had been driven slightly south and taken water nearly to our knees, but we were in good shape except for a few broken shields and the juddering sense of having sailed through the straits of another dimension.

The crew started stroking the oars again, engrossed in conversation about the trials that awaited us; I alone looked up to see the Queen floating down through the rigging lines with the sun's rays bursting around her and the clouds speeding past the sail, her descent so dazzling and dreamlike that I felt as if I were falling upward toward her.

Watching her ease down beside me, I marveled that this was the same woman I had seen sweating poison in her bedchamber. Though dirtied and drenched like the rest of us, she gave off an aura of vitality that ran deeper than flesh, a glow that made me think of the ribbons of light that had caressed me when her hand seized mine and her voice spoke to my inner hearing. In this radiance I could see the Queen, the child who would become a queen, and the doorway to eternity which I had glimpsed as I knelt by her failing body. From the moment she left her sickbed, I had blinded myself to all but the first of these three aspects; the warrior-ruler with pauldrons trimmed in blue silk, and carnelian hair sculpted into a wavy horn in place of a crown.

Yet now it was impossible to ignore her transitory side, not because she showed signs of weakening, but because I had awakened to the vibrant unity of her being... thanks, perhaps, to my own brush with death.

Frowning through streaks of foam-flecked carnelian, she took up her oar and started rowing. I followed suit, and turned my attention to the time-blackened mass domi-nating the coastline, a crudely carved stone formation that resembled the skull of an ape-like creature with the lower jaw missing. Panog's temple thrust itself from the snout's hollow portion, its coal-black battlements crowding the arched cavity like a ravenous jumble of misplaced canine teeth.

Well over a hundred steps ran in narrowing flights from the upper jaw's edge to the flanking towers midway up the shallow slope; yet for all their rough-hewn excess, the temple's arrays, from the fluttering black pennants to the omnivorous castellations, paled in comparison to the overhanging sunken orbs staring blindly seaward, each one twice as large as the temple site and hinting of depths reaching into the monolith's core and perhaps even into the earth itself.

As I fell to picturing what might lie deep within the sooty skull of Mount Verashus, dozens of figures armed with swords and spears began to stream from between the two towers. These doltish puppets of Panog's necromancy, which we half-expected, rushed down the steps and fanned out on the beach, some of them diving into the surf. Since they appeared to number no more than one guard for each of the steps, Kevastra surmised that Panog had dispatched the bulk of his army to Thulam-Kai, one of his rising pupils and servant of Manambal, God of Thrashing Chaos.

"Supposedly this god descended from the Night Gates," she said, with a humorless half-smile, "but neither I nor my scryers have been able to observe it. At any rate, we will see if Panog prefers to overwhelm us or vex us with a small garrison." And then, as if she read my thoughts, for they had turned again, not without some favor, to the living warmth I had felt at her bedside, she added: "Either way, your outcome here is secure. As I ascended above the yellow cloud, I saw a vision of you in the throne room, standing next to Derenna's full-grown daughter. Apparently, I underestimated your part in the plan that I mentioned; just be sure to keep your distance from me once we storm the temple."

Upon finishing this injunction, her golden-green eyes narrowed in sly amusement: "I don't need any special power to recognize your impulses, Danak... but you mustn't jeopardize the work that lies ahead for you."

We continued to barrel toward the shore. Water swamping over our thighs, the oars slicing through the waves, the warriors shouting battle hymns into the winds, our ship on course and pointing straight at the massive set of steps and the loose phalanx of disentombed sea soldiers bobbing toward us. The clouds had veiled the sun's rays again, darkening the foam-capped wilderness and lending the monolith a spectral cast, as if it stood sentinel over the beach at the onset of dusk.

Now the undead skirmishers closed in around the ship, splashing about wildly as they hacked at the hull and prodded their spears at us... for all their frenzy, accomplishing nothing.

It was during this provocation that Kevastra dropped her oar and doubled over. One of the warriors, sitting across from her, jumped from her seat to repel an unseen attacker, only to be chided in a choked voice, "I'm fine, banishing the cloud just tired me a little."

"The venom—" I started to say, stopped cold by the Queen's warning look.

After that, we rowed in silence. I realized I had spoken out of turn. When a child must survive without a parent figure, as she had been forced to do, the attention of others can become an imposition when it involves pointless worry such as I had shown. As we drew closer and closer to the shallows, I drove all thoughts of the poison from my mind. It was one thing to acknowledge our Queen's mortality, quite another to face the facts of her condition as I had observed them at their worst point.

Besides, with the skirmishers harassing us all the way to the shoreline, I had my own worries as the challenges of disembarkation became alarmingly apparent... considering I had never jumped from a boat under fighting conditions.

While it had been ill-mannered of me, in Kevastra's mind, to express my concern for her, it fell upon her without exception to assuage the fears of her companions. In a soft tone—for she must have noted the tremor in my hands as I rowed—she assured me the warriors would make sure I reached the temple safely.

"To be honest, I hadn't thought of how you might help me once we get there," she said, lowering her oar. "But you'll think of something. Just make sure you stay far away from me until I've finished with Panog."

With that, she rose from the water we had taken in and ascended through the rigging lines like a diver coming up for air. Once above the masthead, she floated toward the island as if borne along by some invisible moving path, as motionless as an idol except for her hair blowing in the sea breeze. Our oars lowered, we all watched as the Queen grew faint with distance, gliding over the shore and sweeping up the incline of the prognathic immensity of Mount Verashus.

A skirmisher made me lose sight of her as it bobbed above the gunwale and nearly impaled me; I realized we were entering the shallows and would soon come face-to-face with the main body of our attackers. At this point the warriors all stood and began fending off the growing number of front-line combatants, dispatching as many as they could before the ship was grounded.

At last the keel cut into the sand and Panog's soldiers swarmed around the ship. Fortunately, enough warriors were able to jump out near the stem that we soon managed to divide their assault into melees along the beach, although a handful of us continued to fight them aboard the ship and in the surf.

Though outnumbered, the men and women Kevastra had hand-picked far outmatched the rags of once-human substance that had risen from the deeps to thwart our raid; even my sword found its rhythm as I learned to drive the blundering troops back in the undercurrents. It appeared that as we forced them into smaller groups, they lost sense of how to strike at close quarters.

No blood was shed as our blades sheared through sinew from which all life force had long since emptied into the sea... we became butchers more than fighters as the pathetic dance of steel rolled on. Soon we had finished off the soldiers and set to work berthing the ship on the beach, an accidental monument to the gray, sopping remnants that had been men once strewn in pieces all around it.

The moorings secured, we ascended the upper jaw and began the arduous climb toward the stronghold rising from the black skull's sunken snout. My sword arm was numb and my legs ached, but I kept pace with the others as we raced up the steep wooden steps under Panog's pennants waving beneath a darkening sky. We all kept our eyes on the towers, those with shields raising them against the threat of archers.

No one fired upon us, however, and no more soldiers set upon us, so that we speedily emerged into a courtyard at the top surrounded by a peristyle extending from the two towers to the temple entrance.

It was in this enclosure that a thunderous racket of crashing and rumbling sounded ahead; while at the same time the ground began to shake, prompting us to charge full-speed toward the hulking slab of wood at the far end of the courtyard. The inky half-light gave an impression of sentience in the stone statues fronting the columns on both sides, deities and demons favored by such cabals as the Crucible House.

I half-expected these to beset us as well; yet we reached the cumbersome door unhindered, and stormed into a scene that will haunt me until I cross into the Realms Between... for it was the last time I saw Queen Kevastra alive.

THERE IN THE VAST, shadowy chamber, surrounded by blocks of rubble and bas-relief columns, we came upon her and her adversary locked in a form of combat that I had only read about. They were attacking each other with continuous blasts of energy, hers erupting green fire from her hands, his streaming thunderbolt-brilliance from the wand he brandished on his altar dais. Their energies formed a single undulant cord that glowed according to which blast succeeded at driving back the other.

It did not take long before his thunderbolt stream threatened to surpass her flame-burst; in moments the green fire began to dwindle and flicker as if on the verge of extinguishment. Seeing this, Panog sank into a half-crouch and pointed his wand at the Queen with a double-handed thrust, as if to spear her.

"You're weak, Kevastra!" He crouched lower and twisted the rod in a gesture of prolonged impalement. "Your own arrogance destroys you!"

Incredibly, as his yellow-white light repelled her green flames in a shower of multicolored sparks, the rest of us stood immobilized near the entrance, gaping at the turn the combat had taken. It was not until her hands streaked with thunderbolt flares and her chainmail corset began to smoke that I jolted from the grip of disbelief and darted toward the sorcerer.

My sword raised, I made for the dais in a wide arc, aiming to strike him from behind; I meant to shear him at the waist as he reveled in his vainglorious pantomime, this scrawny, jeering man in a filthy yellow robe who thought to incinerate our Queen with his onyx-studded storm-rod.

Yet as I moved in toward the dais, her voice prodded me to glance in her direction... and I saw her gaze fixed on me, her expression softening from almost motherly anguish to serene understanding. Her mouth moved and her eyes glowed with a white light that gave off twice the luminescence of Panog's lighting-flash. This white light spread over her entire body, drawing the yellow-white currents into itself, while swirls of a dark, vaporous matter grew visible inside it, drifting through the bustling brilliance as if bottled in a jar.

The whole phenomenon so astounded me that I found myself drawing to a halt near the side of the dais.

Then a dread blazed within me as I watched the dazzling halo ripple and swell to such magnitude that her smoking figure seemed like a distant apparition shimmering inside a portal made of quickening star-fire. I could do nothing then as Kevastra turned her full fury upon the final member of the Six Lords... thrusting her hands forward and unleashing a savage radiance like the wrath of a dying sun!

Thankfully, I felt nothing in that moment.

Well, the next I knew, I possessed no sense of myself. My thoughts, if such you could call them, occurred within a darkness that I understood unquestioningly to be the dream of a *shadow* who slept in a realm outside of space and time. As an arising from that dream, I recognized no history, no identity, no agency; I was part of a numinous black emptiness that dreamed itself, abiding in perfect harmony with eternal nothingness.

Little by little, however, I began to detach from the will that dreamed me, as inklings of insufficiency crept into my awareness. And eventually the notion formed that I had been deceived by this will and that I did not belong to a dream of timeless shadow.

On the contrary, I belonged to a world of unrelenting suffering. In that existence, I assumed the identity of someone who had grown profoundly attached to some-one... only to be torn brutally asunder.

Although undefined, the realization struck me with a knowingness that took on qualities I associated with that searing flash of separation. These feelings in turn gave rise to such a discord that what remained of the wholeness of my nonbeing dissolved into the knowledge that I had not only been deceived by the shadow I had thought to be dreaming me, I had been bound by it. From that dissolu-tion a sense of motion and pressure radiated through me that corresponded with certain primitive impulses vaguely associated with my earthly life.

The sensation of heat then began to flare into my dissonant state, intensifying the urgency of the impulses; until at last, the dream grew too faint to sustain the stri-dence building within me, and the darkness exploded into green flames as blinding as the white star-fire I suddenly remembered had consumed my earthly self.

I jerked back into consciousness, calling the name of the one whom I had lost.

"Welcome back," a voice said, somewhere behind me.

In an instant, my bearings returned. I was sprawled on

my back in Panog's temple. My view centered on a bas-relief coiling up one of the columns. It appeared to be an earthworm climbing up the shaft, a ponderous spiral that blended into the capital as if the creature passed through solid matter onto another column on the floor above. For a moment I lay there shuddering at the carving's fat, furrowed ring segments, until I remembered the voice that had followed my cry.

I clambered to my feet and turned toward the source, stumbling about like a drunkard, for I felt as if an anchor hung from my head and my joints had been battered by a blacksmith's hammer.

Once my vision cleared, the speaker impelled me to glance about for my sword; for instead of a member of Kevastra's fighting band, one of Panog's undead soldiers confronted me. It studied me shrewdly even as its head lolled from a deep gash in its neck, its crooked rictus forming a smirk and its skull sockets fired by a vivid red glow. Yet even more repulsive—and confounding—than its incongruous intelligence were the soggy remains of some dozen of its comrades heaped around it, carelessly arranged like carcasses in some shoddy butcher's shop.

"Don't bother, Danak." Its voice bore hints of fall leaves crushed underfoot. "You know me, in a sense. I'm Ral-Bazure; I sheltered your Queen's spirit while you helped her flush the venom out like an overripe fish stew."

My mind raced back to the Queen's healing crisis.

"The Shadow—"

"Let me save you time."

At first, I listened to the monstrosity with disbelief. After all, it could have been one of Panog's tricks, a trap he had set to spring on us in the event of his demise. That made little sense, yet I continued to search about for a sword as the fluent corpse wheezed and sputtered rudely at length, lumbering back and forth among its grisly store of bone, sinew, and rusted armor.

Gradually I relented, however, as the narrative grew increasingly evidential and logical along lines that uniquely suited Kevastra; so that I came to accept the demon's account, even as the devilish itch reclaimed my hands and despair blazed through my insides.

"Your Queen," Ral-Bazure began, "seems to have glimpsed something special about you. That energy she unleashed should have incinerated you in an instant... it certainly had that effect on everyone else inside this architectural absurdity. Nothing more expendable than an elite band of nameless warriors, eh? Apparently, you're the only one with a hand in the grand design.

"Now, stop snarling at me as if you'd like to widen this gouge in my neck; have you already forgotten my oratorical habits? Just hold your tongue and allow me to unravel my narrative in my own fashion. One shouldn't expect sympathy from the shadows, anyway... at least not ones as primeval as mine.

"To the point, then. Not only your nameless warriors, but your Queen as well, have crossed into the Realms Between. The perfidious Panog, too, has evacuated this plane, concomitant with a burst of energy coaxed from that most sparkly of the archdemons, Yeshwan, Torchbearer of the Dawn Gates. Aforementioned radiation wasting all propinquent animate matter and slapping the necromancer's spirit to the Taming Yoke of Eternity, there to serve his vanquisher for, well, eternity.

"It was quite a play: Kevastra glimpsing your part in the grand design, invoking Yeshwan, and annihilating every living being except you within reach. Not to mention sending Panog's venom back to him in the star-blast... all in a span of seconds by your temporal measure. A speedy improvisationalist, Kevastra! And not without a flair, so to speak, for irony.

"As to where I enter into this Thargic tragedy of sorts, after crossing over, she induced me to assist you, much as I had complemented your efforts to drain the poison from her. Whereupon I sheltered you in my Shadow Manteum and recited certain incantations to guide your body through its healing processes—"

"You must want payment for that," I interrupted, stiffening at the memory that I had confused myself with the demon's shadows.

"Already fulfilled." His red orbs brightening, Ral-Bazure indicated his habitation with an ungainly flourish of hand and foot. "As you know from your studies, we higher entities often derive exquisite pleasure from the simpler experiences of, more or less, the flesh. Let's call it less, in this case."

"So you say Kevastra has shifted her focus." I could not get myself to refer to her death directly. "You've spoken to her. Where is she now? *How* is she?"

"Danak, Danak... you know better than to pursue that kind of questioning with me." The demon's head lolled further as his wagging finger crumbled into dust. "*Interesting*... Anyway, as a discorporate being, I operate without reference to terrestrial locations. And my business, you might go so far as to say, overshadows social frameworks. In other words, you speak of a *how* that does not apply to my affairs, nor to anyone else's in what you would call metaphysical existence or the afterlife.

"You might as well ask me if my mother is still having those headaches. I only state the obvious because a certain, shall we say, affliction of the passions has distorted your thinking. What you should really want to know is that the Queen and I exchanged goods and services that... wait... here it—"

With an autumnal chuckle, the desiccated husk that had been Panog's temple guard burst into a billowing cloud of black dust. The explosion chilled my heart and made me question my sanity; as if a long-winded demon addressing me through a mangled corpse were any less strange than the possessed corpse blowing apart.

"Apologies," the same voice wheezed nearby, only to emerge from the settling haze in the remains of another soldier... this one bent from a broad cleft in its side, so that it fixed its luminous red eyes on me in a beggarly posture.

"Consequences are proceeding apace," Ral-Bazure resumed. "Anyway, as I was starting to say, Danak, one thing we have in common with mortals is the predominating principle of exchange. Your Queen and I made a bargain, and by helping you recover from the star-blast, I have kept one-half of it. The other half depends upon my powers of expression to persuade you to abandon these fortifications forthwith."

It was at that moment that my fingers began to itch and my gut seized as if it had caught fire. In one last attempt to deny Kevastra's death, I challenged the demon: "How do I know this is not some illusion cast by either you —if you are you—or Panog? Even granting it's a bit heavy on farce."

"I'll let you decide that. Trust me a moment and turn around. I couldn't harm you in this watery bone sack even if I wanted to."

I ADMIT I did not want to turn around then. I would have preferred to maintain refuge in denial as I had taken shelter in the demon's shadows. Nevertheless, I turned toward the direction that Ral-Bazure indicated with his partially severed finger... and almost wished I had ignored his gesture. For a moment's glance ruined any doubt that the scene could be a deception. Kevastra had indeed broken the Crucible House; her blast had lain waste to every other living being and thrown me some fifty feet across the chamber.

And the battle had indeed taken place as I remembered it, for Panog's temple looked as though it had been assaulted with artillery and a siege engine. Huge chunks of rubble loomed among the wreckage like an accidental mountain range smashed into place by an ill-tempered stone god.

A portion of tumbled bas-relief caught the torchlight blazing from the walls, so that Panog's beloved earthworm appeared to inch along the floor by way of the blood-red glow flickering on its bloated rings. As for the altar itself, only jagged slabs rested on the dais, while smaller fragments lay throughout the piles of ash that covered the floor like residue from a mass funeral pyre... what remained of the men and women I had fought alongside. I knew of their readiness, even their anxiousness, to die for their Queen; yet I felt unworthy as I reckoned the devastation.

And then I noticed the statue a short distance from the altar.

At that moment I heard heavy steps as Ral-Bazure came beside me. My heart thudding, I watched him lumber ahead of me with the arm of a corpse clutched in each hand, dragging his idea of exquisite pleasure toward the altar. His current habitation burst into black dust, however, so that the body on his left struggled to its feet and resumed his labors with the one on the right.

"Come along, Danak," he called in a tortured croak, "and let's see if I can fulfill the second part of my bargain."

I quickly overtook the demon and approached the statue near the altar.

And now you will learn why I sail for home without our Queen's body; for it stood firmly where she had perished, mummified into an ideal of seamless perfection by force of will and star-fire. This projection of her spirit, preserved in stone so smooth it evoked her radiance with dream-like precision, was not without a grim sense of humor.

Kevastra stood with her back to the altar, feet spaced wide, her head cocked back in an expression of sneering triumph. Panog's head dangled from her upraised fist, his hair bunched in her fingers like a long, knotted rag, his thick lips agape, and his eyes rolled back as if an arrow had pierced his forehead. In place of the chainmail corset and leather breeches she had chosen for her final mission, she wore her cuirass, pleated skirt, and pauldrons trimmed in silk; while her hair stood atop her head like a wavy horn again, symbolic of the flame of the Fire Arch.

"Certainly savoring the moment, isn't she?" Ral-Bazure observed, his footsteps ceasing as he released the arm of his habitation-in-waiting. "She seems to think her achievement is quite funny. Almost as if she's considering dropping her trophy into the latrine before relieving herself, wouldn't you say?"

My gut rumbled and my fingers itched viciously as I reached toward the statue's shoulder, hesitated, then stroked the cool, unblemished stone.

Then I started sobbing.

And memories of Kevastra arose unbidden, as if a trapdoor had sprung open in the back of my mind. I thought of how she had looked in her sickbed. I thought of how she had hidden her suffering from the Royal Court, and of how she had hidden it from her warriors, too, as Panog's poison resumed its work inside her. I thought of how she had built a kingdom on the blood of the men who murdered her mother and violated her in childhood.

I thought of all this pain from which she had forged herself, and of how I wanted desperately to return to that period when I had helped her drive the poison from her body. I realized at that moment that I had never really wanted it to end... those seven harrowing days when we had worked in secret toward a hopeless recovery.

As I wept on my knees before the statue, I felt the demon watching me. "I'm well aware of what your primeval shadows think of sympathy," I said. "Leave me alone. Enjoy your simpler experiences of the flesh. You've earned it."

"Remember I haven't fulfilled the second half of my bargain."

I sighed, choked down tears. "I'm waiting."

"I told your Queen I would make sure you got off the island."

"I refuse to even think about that right now."

Ral-Bazure burst out laughing, and then burst into a pile of dust.

"Danak, you may have noticed the acute impermanence of these bone sacks," the demon said, speaking through the second body he'd dragged with him. "Panog not only mastered the art of restoring the dead to a pretense of living, he wielded the power to force organic matter into rapid states of deterioration. Judging from what I've observed up here and down on the beach, he appears to have arranged for such a process to commence immediately upon any marked changes in his condition... of which metamorphosing into an engrossing piece of sculpture certainly counts. A means of getting the last word, so to speak, with his conquerors.

"Now, that alone should motivate you to get back to your ship and make the Queen's sigils—located among the ballast—speed you home. But there is a further complication, as is usually the custom with blackhearted sorcerers. And this would be—"

Just then one of the corpse's legs exploded, so that it dropped to one knee and pitched sideways in its own powder-burst.

"—that the rate of deterioration appears to be accelerating," Ral-Bazure resumed, his voice strained and faint with distance, as another habitation pulled itself to its feet among the bodies he had relocated from the shore. Again dragging a corpse on either side of him, he made his way back to the altar, wobbling and stumbling in a strenuous sequence of narrowly avoided falls.

His red orbs flickering from the exertion, he released his spare habitations and lumbered toward me.

"I don't seem to be deteriorating," I said, holding my arms out for inspection. But the demon ignored me.

"Naturally, or rather unnaturally," he went on, "not all vulnerable materials will decay at the rate of hapless seafarers nefariously recalled from the deeps. But unless you're made of steel or stone, Danak, you are not immune to the principle of disintegration that Panog has set in motion here. Therefore you must hasten back to the *Champion* before you cease to be... well, to be. Save your plashy ululations for the voyage home."

I climbed to my feet and faced Kevastra's statue. "Fine. We'll leave soon. And you're going to help me get her onto the ship."

"We? Preposterous! I'm staying here until I've run out

of bone sacks with which to amuse myself. And you can't take her with you, Danak. I don't know how you survived a Yeshwanian star-blast, but you stood a better chance of that than budging your Queen's parting gesture to the Crucible House. A monument made of star-fire cannot be damaged and will remain where it stands for all time.

"Which, on that note, is a commodity that continues to slip away the longer you fix your mournful gaze upon an adventure that never belonged to you. If you stay here much longer, your teary cheeks will turn to dust and *poof!* Then it may be weeks, perhaps months, before a search party arrives here, only to—"

Poof!

Once again, Ral-Bazure willed another corpse to rise and brightened his red orbs at me as if he had more than adequately made his point.

"Perhaps whatever happened to me has thwarted the decaying process," I said.

"'Hand in the grand design,' as previously acknowledged. But for that very reason you don't want to test your flesh against Panog's necromancy; too many unknowns there. The last of the Six Lords may have been a lesser mage, but only by Kevastra's standards. And not even she knows whether or to what extent you can resist his curse, else she would have informed me."

Raising one arm stump in an acknowledging gesture, the demon plodded toward me.

"But perhaps the star-blast did give you some defense against instant disintegration. Or perhaps my healing incantations are impeding it. Or perhaps the onset of the *poof!* manifests differently in a living being—you *are* feeling out of sorts, are you not? A detestable burning in the hands and belly? What if these symptoms indicate that you are only slightly more resistant than my bone sacks? By the way, Danak, wool decays, too, and not even your Queen's sigils can maneuver a ship without a working sail."

"Well, at least give me some space to observe a vigil, then. If there are to be no burial rites, I deserve that much."

"'If it were up to me...' as they say. But these are Kevastra's orders. You are aware that a new cabal is on the rise? Little has been discovered about this organization, as it seems to possess an unprecedented skill in concealing itself from scryers on this plane or any other. All anyone knows is that it is led by Thulam-Kai, Panog's greatest pupil, and that he worships an abomination known as Manambal."

"Give me some time alone with her and I will do as you tell me. The ship will sail... it has to."

With that, I turned my back on the demon and contemplated the statue's sneering visage. Thinking back to Kevastra's vow to "part Panog's head from his bony little body," I felt myself smile for the first time in a long while... until a hand closed on my arm. "The grand design," the raspy voice grated in my ears. "No doubt it involves Thulam-Kai and his mystery deity. You have to go now—"

As the demon's damp, skeletal grip tightened, I felt the inner heat that had been racking me shoot like a flash of star-fire behind my eyes.

"*Get off of me!*"

I shrugged him off with my arm. The motion not only loosened Ral-Bazure's hold, it sent him flying back toward the heap of corpses. His habitation crashed down some thirty feet across the chamber, shattering like an absurd funerary vase and scattering bony fragments through the piles of ash.

The other corpse near the altar pulled itself to its feet. "Well now, it seems you *have* acquired some abilities," the demon said. "This genuinely arouses my curiosity. Further investigation seems in order..."

I agreed. And rather than obsess with mourning rites, I turned my thoughts to the miracle of why I was alive.

Kevastra had mentioned receiving a vision of me; she had seen me standing in the throne room next to Derenna's full-grown daughter. And several times she had spoken of a larger plan in which she came to realize I played a significant part. Of course, it stirred my passions, as the demon called them, to draw on these incidents as the basis for envisioning myself as some sort of savior; a champion, furthermore, whom the Queen foresaw as an emergent force in our kingdom's destiny. For that reason, fearing vanity and self-delusion, I had thought little about my impossible survival except in relation to Panog's curse.

Now, however, I could no longer ignore Kevastra's sacrifice as an act that triggered some powerful transformation within me. And although I could not say why, I felt the key to this change lay within the few words she had spoken to me. Yet even as I realized this much, I still began to question whether my removal of Ral-Bazure had been a chance occurrence.

It was almost comical the way the demon lumbered back and forth, his red orbs flaring and dimming as he regarded me intently, perhaps with a touch of apprehension that I might transplant him an even further distance without having to lay hands on his habitation. Then, as he emerged from behind the dais, he kicked up a gray cloud as something scraped underfoot; bending down, he pulled my sword from the ashes and raised it with what struck me as an attitude of challenge, not without a sense of amusement.

"It seems that sails and bone sacks are not the only items subject to deterioration," I said, nodding at the blade, which had rusted from base to point.

And then the rumbling started.

At first it sounded like distant thunder, and for a moment I wondered if the curse had not also caused the weather to turn. Then I realized the noise was carrying from somewhere within Mount Verashus, perhaps one of the giant eye sockets projecting above the battlements of Panog's stronghold. The longer this went on, the louder and more distinct the booming grew, rolling through the core of the monolith like fast-approaching thunder claps.

Soon I could distinguish between the crashing of swift strides and the bellowing cries of some enraged creature; it had to be gigantic, judging by how the walls began to shake, and it was heading in our direction, bounding at a speed that sounded like cannonballs hammering down on the floor above us.

Breathless, I barely noticed my companion as he came to a lurching halt beside me. In speechless amazement, we both stared at the ceiling as the thunderous din swelled to a cataclysmic roar some thirty feet from us, in the opposite direction of the corpses. Chunks of stone rained down from the ceiling then, as the beast started pummeling the floor where it stood.

The blows rattled the walls like a confused charge of battering rams in the heart of a thunderstorm. Then the ceiling finally gave way, rupturing in a deafening burst that rocked the great chamber in a downpour of dust and enormous stone fragments; from the breach something gargantuan and grotesquely human-like descended, quickly obscured by the dark cloud that mushroomed up from the wreckage, blotting out everything for several heartbeats.

"Give me my sword," I heard myself say.

A few of the torches blazed on through the dust blast. These threw a tremulous red light on the massive head and shoulders that became visible as the air cleared, so that the creature's eyes lit up like Ral-Bazure's in his borrowed forms. And now we saw what the black skull would have looked like in the fullness of flesh when beasts the size of Mount Verashus dominated the earth. Only this creature belonged to no class of ape such as they were known to exist in any period... and not because of his mountainous proportions.

For he did not rest on his knuckles, but rather stood on his hind legs, waving his upper limbs in rhythmic undulations; these were the living expressions of Panog's earthworm as depicted on the bas-relief columns! Fat and glistening, the ring segments that formed each arm were a bright blood-red, and needed no firelight to give the impression of serpents dancing at the mouth of hell.

As the last of the cloud faded away, we saw what had caused the beast to show himself after remaining silent for so long. Rust had eaten into the runes engraved on his restraints, so that he had snapped the enchanted chains that bound him and chased down the only scent of life within the monolith. Down one shoulder hung the broken chain that had secured the manacle around his neck, while from the midpoint of his fettered limbs the useless metal bands swung like flails through the faint red haze of the torchlight.

With a growl, he swept away the debris piled around him; the huge slabs smashed into the columns on either side as if flung by catapults as tall as himself. Then, as more dust and stone fragments showered down from the ceiling, his earthworm-limbs reared like cornered vipers to reveal scarlet mouths rimmed by black, sickle-shaped teeth.

And while the pageantry of horrors went on, I wondered again if I were losing my sanity; for rather than succumb to the revulsion of my ancestors, I began to examine the creature and noticed signs of the curse to which he, too, had fallen prey. I even heard myself laugh, noting his patchy fur and shriveled belly, as if someone else were enjoying these marks of weakness through my eyes.

"Give me my sword," I told Ral-Bazure again, holding out my hand.

Waving his earthworm-limbs again, the ape-like behemoth bent low on his dais of fractured stone and sounded a squall of hateful fury. The mingled growl and ragged shriek pounded through my skull as if I stood inside a demon-haunted church bell tolling at the midnight hour. Still, for the first time since I had awakened after the star-blast, my hands tingled rather than burned, and the fiery knots in my gut gave way to a sharp and anxious hunger, even as the sulfurous odor of carrion breath wafted toward us.

A giddy feeling welled up within me, not unlike the calm I had experienced by Kevastra's sickbed, only fluttery and urgent; while my heart beat as if it might burst, spurred by an elation I had never known.

The creature roared again, and sent another tremor through the chamber as his earthworm-limbs smote the floor like the signal of a war drum.

"Give me my sword," I told the demon yet again, and this time the gritty leather grip slipped into my hand.

"Danak, I cannot advise you to take a rusted sword to a gigantic, eldritch monster fight," Ral-Bazure cautioned. "There are no doubt alternate exits that you may discover with perseverance, if you would but turn and hasten your passions in the opposite direction."

"Your primeval shadows are showing signs of sympathy, O Lord of Shadows."

"You must be confusing me with another demon. I am only trying to fulfill my bargain."

I gazed upon Kevastra's statue once more. Her upraised eyes smiled with the foreknowledge that she would never be defeated; not by sorcery, not by history, and certainly not by death itself.

The eternal Queen of the Fire Arch.

"Don't worry, Ral-Bazure... we will get through this."

WELL, some of you might suppose my courage left me the moment I dashed headlong toward the creature. And you would be right. I'm not even sure I had a plan of attack, unless I had thought to slay him by throwing my sword at some vital weak spot, as so often occurs in heroic tales. It was as if Kevastra's statue had elevated my energy like a healing stone, infusing me with an almost drunken sense of possibility and purpose.

The further I drew away from it, however, the more I felt myself awaken, as I had when I broke free from Ral-Bazure's shadows; suddenly I lost all instinct except to dart about aimlessly and make useless calculations. Had I been the creature looking down upon me, I might have supposed the little man to have stumbled into a tunnel of cobwebs teeming with spiders. Meanwhile, the demon's strained, unintelligible shouts behind me did nothing to sharpen my focus.

For a while, the beast let me skirt around him. Now and then his earthworm-limbs would descend and crawl along the floor to drive me the other direction. Yes, he was toying with me... and yet I knew if I turned and fled the way I had come, he would either pulverize me or snatch me up and fling me like a pebble.

At one point, it occurred to me to take cover against

the stone slab on which he stood, for it exceeded my height in thickness; but he must have sensed my plan as I hesitated, for he lashed his earthworm-limb down and carved a trough in the floor that fractured the slab and ended a few feet in front of me. Thus foiled by this mocking act, I realized I could do nothing but react to his feints and watch my fate unfold in graceful, serpentine shapes high above me.

With mesmerizing elegance, the monstrous whips of fat, blood-red rings danced ever closer to me, until I ceased to retreat or raise my sword in defense. But at last, one of them slashed down at tremendous speed, and my free hand shot out by some ridiculous reflex, as if I thought I could drive it back with a beam of flame, as Kevastra might have done.

And the creature froze.

At first, I took it for another feint; but then I realized that I, too, stood powerless to move. My hand would do nothing but remain outstretched, poised to fire an immaterial blast at the ring of black teeth yawning over me. Yet for all the panic suspended in that gesture, I now felt weightless and insensate, detached from my impending death as if I saw it from a greater vantage point... a source of higher intelligence that suddenly swept me into itself and allowed me to observe and receive vast stores of information instantaneously... the knowledge of a thousand books in a single moment!

My mind, of course, could not organize or retain the flood of wonders. But then Kevastra appeared just as I despaired that I would lose the answers I had longed to know all my life, and I knew she was speaking to me right before she unleashed the star-blast; I saw her as clearly as if I stood within the white light that had flared in her eyes and swelled into the magnificent halo that would consume her.

"You nursed me," she told me. "You burned for me, Danak! You are always burning... *burn brighter.*"

And in a flash of understanding, I knew... what I needed to know.

I had avoided annihilation because a part of our leader lived on in me. When she had grasped my hand at the height of her healing crisis, she had unwittingly passed a spark of her eternal self between us. Panog's poison may have overcome her already worn defenses, but my own health had been illumined by the gift of her grace, so that I possessed the strength to withstand the star-blast. Not only that, the light of the Dawn Gates was an aspect of the ultimate energy that formed the basis of the Realms Between and enmeshed all beings and operations within its field of intention.

This meant that when the star-blast struck me, the powers of both sorcerers, Queen Kevastra and Panog, *became enmeshed in my own range of influence upon this plane of existence.* Their energies and abilities, their mastery of spellwork, were now mingled within me; and by that joining I was bound to serve Kevastra's successor in the role that had been laid out for me between this higher intelligence and the tension of forces on earth.

As I relate this after the fact, I am well aware that some of you still believe me to be both delusional and guilty of blasphemy. This is understandable, for you base your judgments on practical experience of human behavior... and not on *direct* experience of information passed through means beyond the constraints of social necessity or rational thought.

It is imperative that I change your minds when I return. But until then, know that while I belonged to the higher intelligence and its flow of lucidity, I lost any desire to question or deny what I was presented in the interest of self-protection. For not only did I embrace my reinvention as a sorcerer of the Royal Court, I was shown an elaborate vision that warned of a threat even greater than the Crucible House in the rise of Panog's pupil, Thulam-Kai... whose master, Manambal, God of Thrashing Chaos, I was mercifully spared the memory of glimpsing once I descended from my vantage point to the dreary horrors of Panog's temple.

The head full of black teeth resumed its swing toward me. Yet the earthworm-limbs were nothing compared to what I had seen in my half-remembered vision of the enemies on the horizon. From my outstretched hand an inky-black beam erupted, enveloping the slimy appendage and causing it to *poof* as easily as one of Ral-Bazure's habitations. As the creature screamed in rage and agony, I floated up toward the ceiling in a vertical position like Kevastra, and, hovering on a level with his face, swiped another beam across his chest, so that his torso and legs disintegrated and cascaded to the floor in a waterfall rush of silvery-black dust.

Next, I transmuted my rusted sword into a blade of green flame as long as the earthworm-limbs and parted the beast's head from his gigantic, eldritch shoulders. His head and shoulders went *poof* with another blast of inky-black, while his other arm fell to the floor with a bloody plop that struck me as comical... although the wave of amusement did not entirely feel like my own. Then, as the dust billowed up in another mushroom cloud, I turned and floated back toward the ruins of Panog's altar.

I set down before the Queen's statue and gazed upon her again, marveling at the force of her will as mummified in star-fire.

And I knew then that Queen Kevastra would always watch over us... she *is* the Fire Arch.

Undefeated. Eternal. Indomitable.

"Congratulations on your apotheosis," I heard Ral-Bazure wheeze.

"I am not a god," I said. "Although I can make you go *poof* at will."

"As you have been all along. For which I must give thanks, for you have provided me exquisite entertainment in these bone sacks."

"How long have you known?"

The demon fixed his red orbs on my sword, so I handed it to him.

"Interesting... so you can reverse the *poof* effect, too? How far do your new powers extend, Danak?"

"I don't know. But answer me: How long have you known that I was causing certain types of matter to disintegrate?"

"Well, as I mentioned, after you gently removed my arm, I decided your situation warranted further research. So, while you stood motionless in your best impersonation of Kevastra, minus the actual lethal rainbow blast, I struck some bargains in various higher dimensions and learned that *you* were somehow accelerating the breakdown of organic matter—not that you were aware of this—owing to a disagreement between certain passions within your breast and the bothersome problem of impermanence." For a moment, Ral-Bazure froze, as if bracing for another change of habitations.

"Please don't soften your sarcasm on my account," I said.

"Fine. I did not, however, obtain any information concerning your battery of new abilities, much less how you came to acquire them."

"I'm surprised she didn't warn you about the *poof* effect

first... given certain things I learned while you were making inquiries about me."

"Perhaps she underestimated your loyalty, Danak. Or perhaps the grand design enjoys misdirection at certain junctures. In any case, it seems you can stay here as long as you like, now. You certainly won't have any problems if another of Panog's pets comes out of hiding."

"No. You were right about Manambal and his mystery deity. It's time for me to sail home. And you should be glad, too... for you have fulfilled your end of the bargain."

I turned toward Kevastra's statue one last time. In a sense, I felt I had completed my vigil over what remained of her; I hoped she was proud of me for accomplishing as much.

"I will always burn for you," I said.

"A Thargic tragedy," Ral-Bazure said.

I turned away from the statue finally, and headed for the steps that would lead me back to the island.

THERE... now you have heard everything. For the moment, I don't expect you all to believe it. But I do expect you to prepare the troops, in secret, anyway, until the time is right to announce the Queen Regent.

Regardless of what you think of me for the time being, a second war of the cabals is coming.

And by the way, I *do* know what all of you are thinking, at least to some degree. Through means I don't quite understand yet, I can sense the vibration of your passions through the oculus of the Black Pool. And the vibration tells me that you are afraid.

You are afraid that I speak the truth. You are afraid that we cannot survive without Queen Kevastra to lead us.

But you will soon see: A part of her lives on in me. In *all* of us. For we are the Fire Arch... undefeated, eternal, and indomitable.

We will burn as bright as the Dawn Gates. We will continue to build Kevastra's vision of prosperity and enlightenment. I was a teacher before I met our kingdom's founder, and I will be one again.

But for now, we must fight.

THE SONG OF THE NAMELESS PHALLUS

EDWIN CALLIHAN

I

"Take your pick." Rigora pulled back a purple curtain revealing multitudes of naked flesh, posed and exposed like disrobed mannequins and primed for lust.

"Doesn't matter," the new, nameless customer dismissed, switching his gaze to the bar.

Rigora ran a small bordello at the outskirts of Dim, a haven for drunk mercenaries, disgraced demagogues, and simple bastards but this particular individual was a challenge for her to read. He was a robust man clothed in a black hood and g'lac skin, looming with the night's menace as his companion. Old scars decorated his visible flesh like a travelog of wickedness. And within these impressions of unknown violent past, there was a fresh wound, slashed right across his chest.

Rigora stared at the lacerations, weeping red, debating if they were claw marks or the carvings of a dull blade. The shape of the wound reminded her of the constellations, contrived with intersecting lines that mirrors a majestic scene from the night sky. Before she could mention cleaning himself up, he covered it up with his cloak.

Rigora assumed him a wounded savage, defenseless like a sawtooth with a broken jaw but still strong enough to sever spines. She remained non-threatening and docile, easing her way behind the bar.

His only personal effect besides the clothes on his back was a burlap sack clutched in his massive fist.

"Leave your weapons at the bar." Rigora demanded. "You'll get 'em back come morning."

"I have none," the man said. His voice, tired and hoarse.

"Ain't safe to be wandering around here without a blade."

He didn't say anything.

Rigora left her curiosity and reluctance to the silence of her skull. She was not interested in personal details, only coins that spent. If he couldn't pay, he couldn't stay.

The man paced anxiously up the bar, examining the barrels. "I want a gourd of pale water, too. The strongest you got."

Rigora started to open her mouth to hit the man with the price but before she could speak he yanked a handful of colorful jewels and slapped them on the bar top. The jewels jingled like windchimes and lit up the dusky bordello in spectral emanation. Rigora's jaw slacked and she smiled.

"Olna!" Rigora summoned, furiously.

"Yes, Madame." Olna said. She bored between the other nude employees of the bordello. Her black hair obscured her chest until she wrapped herself in a translucent robe knitted from Jogu webbing.

"You're up," Rigora said. "Escort the new guest to your corridor."

"Of course," Olna said. "Follow me, um..." She

waited for the man to share his name, but he remained silent, frowning.

Rigora chuckled, counting the jewels, and vanished behind a buttress as the two ascended the spiraling staircase. Olna had never slept with a man of this size before, and as of late, business is much slower, so perhaps this man was a blessing.

"Please, hurry." The man gently shoved her, his hands like paws of a forest beast.

"Forgive me."

Olna opened the door to her room, lit a lamp and leaped to the bed. The springs in the mattress squeaked. "The bed is sturdy, trust me," Olna said, giggling. "See." She hopped up and down, her breasts in sync with gravity.

The man entered and eyeballed the contents of the room.

"Is everything to your liking?" Olna ceased bouncing and watched him move about the space.

The man hung his cloak on the bedpost and secured his burlap sack on a table at his bedside. His head was freshly shaved, an odd style for a traveler, but Olna paid no mind. She wasn't shallow, as long as his parts worked right.

He rushed to the open window, peeking outside. The rain pattered, the ocean laughing beyond Dim's borders. He looked up, letting the rain hit his face, and sighed with relief. He knew the storm would obscure the stars' guidance.

For the night.

"What are you looking at?" Olna asked, confused.

"Nothing." He parked next to her and raised his gourd to his lips, gulping like an exhausted g'lac in the watering hole.

"Thirsty?"

He nodded, and laid back on the bed like it was a cloud.

She threw her leg over his lap and straddled him.

"What's your name? I like to know so I can scream it."

"My name?" He lifted his head. It reminded her of a talking skull. "It makes no difference. Call me whatever you wish. I'm here to drink and copulate and, most of all, sleep." He gazed at the window for a moment. "Let's not complicate the evening with kinship."

"Lord, what happened?" Olna gasped.

"I am tired," He clenched his fist. "Perhaps more pale water will help elevate my mood."

"Yes. May I have a drink?" Olna asked. "Might loosen us both up. I'm not used to customers like you."

"Like me?"

"Our patrons aren't typically from beyond the borders of Dim." Olna generously sipped from the gourd a few times, the tickle turned to a burn in her throat. "Where are you from?"

"Far away."

"I bet you have many stories."

"Yes, many." The man's voice simmered like cooled magma, his shoulders deflated, and he started to grin.

"Tell me," Olna said, her eyes, saurian and swirling. She got up on her knees, behind him, and started massaging his shoulders. "Tell me what you've seen. Tell me about your wounds." She begged.

The pale water is sweet like syrup, thin and easy to drink. It doesn't take long for the effects to take charge. They both feel their essence torn from their physical bodies and glide back down like a feather. Reality sprouted invisible cilia that crawled across their skin. They sat and watched lamp-light go from a moody flicker to strobes of tiny star bursts.

"Which one?" He finally responded, scanning his arms for scars.

"How about..." She paused as she ran her finger

across his chest, she could feel his heart thump melodically, and stopped at his newest wound. "This one."

"This one? I'm weary to orate such a strange encounter."

"Tell me." It was no longer a mere suggestion, it was a demand under the intoxication of such strong pale water.

The man leapt from the bed, like a prowling feline, slashing the air with an invisible saber.

Olna cackled and clapped, bouncing again on the bed.

"Listen." He shushed her, slurring his words.

II

"My travels led me down many paths. I've taken the lives of many men, I've defeated numerous abominations that creep beyond your borders, and sailed between the shores of Urthoch and Mgo. Undispellable violence and blood-lust, you must understand. And come late was no doubt my most challenging.

"You see, I ascended upon a village several days ago. The twin suns still hung above, slowly sinking behind the hills. This village was welcoming back the fathers that worked in the jewel mines, but there was no celebration for their long season's fruitful labors. The men had returned to an unholy spectacle. Their children, motherless and crying into oblivion, roaming the streets like walking skeletons. Many of the infants were already small corpses lying in cribs. The fathers were helpless cowards, I suppose. They saw me as some sort of messiah to usher them through this dawning age of darkness."

"What happened?" She asked. The flames of the lamp crackled in the humidity.

"All the mothers vanished."

"Vanished?" Thunder rumbled and the lamp's flame

fluttered like bat wings in a gust of wind but remained lit, casting long shadows against the walls.

"Yes, all of them," he continued. "Vanished leaving behind only footprints. The fathers, of course, blamed their misfortune on forgotten prayers to their god."

"Who did they pray to?" She asked.

"I don't know," He scoffed. "I do not bother myself with false gods. There is only one true terrestrial power." He veered off on a senseless philosophical tangent. The effects of pale water can vary. Olna held back a yawn until she found the right opportunity to shift the focus back to the missing mothers.

"And they were certain the mothers had not been killed or kidnapped?"

"Were you listening, wench?" he snarled. "Footprints, I said. There were footprints that led to the hills."

"Why didn't the father's search for them?"

"These weak men had no spines. At one point, the fathers were on their knees, crying upon the muddy footprints of their missing women. Some insisted they heard the mothers singing beyond the trees." He chuckled, "Pathetic. Even their Rector was just as delusional, mumbling on a mind trip as he nursed a jug of pale water, I suppose to replace his dead newborn. He was certain that while they mined the jewels this season, a sorcerer had traveled across the celestial gulf of infinity on the tail of a moonbeam far beyond any star we could see, coming to explore our world and reap what pleasures populate our fauna.

"I assumed they were drunk but the fathers offered me quite a handsome reward to investigate the matter. So, I grabbed my sword and followed the footprints for the rest of the day, trudging through the exotic fungi, moss, and rotten wood. And I eventually stumbled upon a massive clearing in the woods. An oblong crater of some sort, which made me question the validity of the Rector's claim, but it was as if the trees had not grown in the spot for centuries. There wasn't even a blade of grass or a weed sticking out of the soil. Just dirt and a single altar right in the middle of it all."

"An altar?" Olna asked while the man chugged more of his pale water.

"Yes, an altar unlike any I had ever seen. There were no symbols or motifs to attach it to any known religion or cult that I've encountered. It was deep rooted into the ground and made of some chromium metallurgy that reflected the world's gaze. A spectacular microcosm of architecture."

"What did you do?"

"I waited," he said, drinking more. "Until I hear the singing."

"Singing?"

"Yes, it was a merry tune, not my particular kind of melody, but they seemed to quite enjoy it."

"Who?"

"The mothers. And they were not leading this choir, however. No, it was an androgynous voice, singular and many, mighty and like a whisper, all at once. When I looked at the women, none of their mouths were open, and their eyes were scooped out of their heads. They danced to the song in a loose formless motion, gradually intertwining with each other's arms and legs. I continued to watch them from afar, keeping my presence unknown for my own pleasure. They moved to the ground, their naked bodies fornicating like an undulating mass of serpents during breeding season."

"Who was singing?"

"Nobody was. That's what puzzled me. I figured it was the mere trickery of a freak magician but my conclusion was vapid. Yet, I noticed one of them placed a strange device upon the altar. A shining chromium phallus that bloomed like the cap of a phosphorescent toadstool. It appeared to have a face in the depressions of its top. The longer I stared, the more it seemed to grow, triumphing the size of a g'lac femur. The mothers moaned before it. The phallus pulsed, and spit out an alarming screech, tendrils shot from it, twisting and writhing like worms, taking a shape, a form! Like the contours of what appeared to be a man. The phallus crested in between the newly formed legs. It was an orgy of madness, a mockery of life. The mothers bowed as it screamed like something not of our world into the black void above, under pillars of light from the moons and stars.

"The face took shape and I locked eyes with the abomination. It felt like I was looking in a mirror. A crude imitation of myself.

"One of the mothers rose up and took to the altar and engaged with the phallus in the most vile manner. And I must admit, I turned away, no longer interested in any pleasures the scene could afford me. It was then I knew what I had to do." He imitated slicing his throat with a blade.

"You killed them?" Olna asked, sitting back down on the bed.

"I had to," he said. "They were no longer wives or mothers. They were mutants in servitude to whatever filth they worshiped at that altar."

"How? You mentioned you had a sword but I did not see you check any weapons with Rigora."

"Are you insisting that I am lying?" He edged up to her like a rabid jackal cornering prey.

Olna shook her head.

"I couldn't just return the mothers to their normal lives, they were tainted with the most unholy consummation. So, I sent them to the deepest of graves."

She said nothing. She knew he was right. There is no place for undesirables like her or him, that is why they live destitute and among the negative space. Among lawlessness and barbarism. She was no different than the eyeless whores and he was no different than whatever was at that altar. They all operated between the ground they walked and the realm of celestial bodies that hung above them, careless and indifferent.

It was silent. The man breathed heavily at the end of the bed, staring out the windows at the rain beat down and the wind roared.

"I'm tired. Now let's fuck and sleep."

"But you never told me about your wound. How did you get it?"

He didn't say anything.

"The bag," Olna said. "It's in there isn't it?"

He clutched her throat and she levitated from the bed. "Do not trouble yourself with what I carry. It is mine, and only mine. I have paid your Madame what is due, nothing more, and this will be the end of it okay? I'd heed my warning, wench, or this might be your last fuck." He was spitting when he talked now. The point of pale water intoxication that could either lead men to violence or lust.

Olna nodded, gasping for air, clawing at his fist.

"Good. Now, finish me off." He released her and dropped her on the bed like a straw doll.

Olna turned over and the savage man mounted her. He attempted to thrust himself against her several times but he felt limp. Olna snorted, trying to hold back laughter, his prick felt like nothing on her bare ass, like skin against skin. She looked back, to see him hunch over himself, snoring, wrapped in a blanket.

She laid there beside him, watching his chest rise and fall. The fresh wound seemed old now. Scabbed with dark plasma and crust, like black mold and spores.

The gourd of pale water was on the floor, she knocked back the last swigs and tossed it.

The bag called to Olna and curiosity took hold. She just wanted to peek, to see if the story he told had any truth to spare. Better yet, maybe it was a lie, it was full of coin or jewels, she could convince Rigora to tax this savage for his unkindness if he tries to cheap out.

Olna opened it like it was a precious gift, slowly folding back the opening, and reached in. She pulled out the handle of a broken sword, snapped in the middle as if it were a twig or a hollow bone.

She felt let down, disappointed that what the man had recounted was only the ramblings of a limp dick drunk.

But then, she heard it sing.

At first, it was just in her head and in an alien tongue but it became clearer and understandable the more she listened.

And there it was on the bed, glowing like a solar flare.

Waiting for Olna.

It moved.

It lived.

She gripped the large metallic phallus like pulling a sword from its sheath. It squirmed like a giant slug, flailing back and forth between her fingers.

A depressed face in the cap, stretching its craw like a dying fish, hitting notes off the scales.

It sang to her.

A song for Olna.

She was paralyzed by its song,

It leaped from her hands and crawled in a trail of slime, her legs a bridge to her worldly flesh.

An ancient melody of the future. Thorned empires grown from crystalline formation and sentient fungi.

Between the cracks of the void.

A throne was waiting for her.

Olna ascended through the ceiling like a ghost. At first it was lonely and cold. The darkness of the heavens wrapped around her like she was an infant. She looked for her hands and feet but they were gone. Without a body, without weight, without mass her essence continued to climb closer to the vastness of the void. Olna thought it was twinkling stars but as she drew closer she realized how wrong her perception had been.

The thousand breasts of a sleeping celestial creature, sagged from its titanic body, dripping with ethereal milk. Olna yearned for a taste, to suck on it like it was her own mother. She latched to the teet and consumed.

It moaned.

Or maybe it was Olna in her dream.

And it erupted.

III

Olna woke up on the ground, her head thumping like a newly formed crater.

She rose in the peeking rays of dawn and tapped the savage man to rise from the bed.

"Hey." She tapped. "Time's up. Tips go by the bed, and Rigora will see you out."

The man didn't move. His stillness, belonging to a catacomb.

Olna rolled him over, and yanked the blanket off, and realized he was in fact a corpse. His muscle mass depleted into dry skeletal decay. The once smooth flesh was now crinkled like dried fruit in the sun. There were no eyes, his nose was gone, and his teeth protruded from the mouth of a fully formed skull. Between his legs was a gaping hole, without a penis, it had been stolen.

She forgot to scream, instead she thought about the Phallus from last night.

The dream, the hallucination, the vision, the explorations of the macrocosms of being and unbeing.

Between the cracks.

Olna couldn't leave it. She wanted it back for herself; needed it.

She thrusted the savage man's corpse off the bed and it dissipated into tiny spores, falling between the floorboards and crevices like an hourglass.

But this did not concern Olna, she only wanted one thing and with her strength lifted the bed from the floor, only to find nothing.

She leaped down the stairs to an empty bordello.

"Rigora!" She screamed "Rigora!"

No answer.

There was nobody.

But she heard the singing.

It never stopped.

And she would never stop looking for it.

She would take the lives of many men, defeat numerous abominations that creep beyond borders, and sail between the shores of Urthoch and Mgo. Undispellable violence and bloodlust, you must understand. And come late was no doubt the most challenging.

LIGHT FROM A DEAD STAR
SAM RICHARD

Beneath twin moons, the earth fought against the brittle metal of Taura's shovel. Hard packed soil, full of stone and dead roots. She kept digging. Like a machine: unstopping, rusty and jagged and cold. By the time the hole revealed itself in the earth the morning sun had broken past the horizon, warming her sweat-drenched face.

Soil stuck to her arms in a second skin like armor. The gift of the grave. A kiss from beyond before the true and final embrace.

Palmier's body was rigid and cool; wounds glistening in the morning light. If there was room for tears Taura would have given them to the earth. Would have given them to Palmier. But there was no room. No time. No anything.

Only unceasing rage. Unbridled heartbreak. Unknowable change. A storm inside with no outlet.

She lowered her lover's body into the ragged grave, kissing them on the forehead and then cheeks and then finally lips. Cold, unmoving lips.

Cold.

Unmoving.

It shook through her and the rage broke for a moment, allowing a few tears to escape her eyes and drop into wounds, which swallowed up the salty fluid like life's blood.

Gently she filled the grave with the steaming soil. Wisps of vapor trailed from the pile and diffused into the heavy dampness of the morning light. As she covered Palmier's body, Taura imagined them too diffusing; perhaps becoming a part of a larger world. A grander story. A more beautiful whole.

The idea was seductive. She suddenly wanted to throw herself into the burial plot and become one with nothing and everything in such a terrible and beautiful way, but an arm was wrapped around her emotions. One of vengeance and retribution and a thousand hearts cut silent by war and hatred and loyalty and Taura's own hand.

A hand that begged to caress her axe. A hand that begged to wrap itself around the throat of those who killed this perfect, kind, gentle, hilarious soul. A hand that was thirsty for not just blood to spill, but to feel that very blood run until the earth was soaking.

A hand that ached under the weight of so much soil. The heaviest soil.

When she was done, Taura watched the rising of the sun, and the cascading of rays upon her lover's grave, and she prayed to the God of Scars for the first time in decades. She prayed for vengeance. She prayed for blood and accepted the price.

She accepted the scars demanded of her. Scars that would join a map of pain across her body now ages old. A map untouched for half a lifetime.

Her joints and muscles ached, pulling her to the warm soil atop the grave. She fell into sleep, giving into the sorrow. New tears flowing into the earth, helping feed the hungry mouths of disrupted sprouts and seeds. As she drifted, she hoped that one day those same sprouts could bring life to the monument of death. To bring something good out of so much suffering.

In her final conscious thoughts, Taura's body jolted with tension, as she saw the eyes of gods long forgotten, and the price of remembering. She also saw the eyes of another skulking in the shadows. Someone gnarled and unknown but familiar. Someone watching with unnatural strength and shimmering crystal teeth that dripped thick, clear fluids.

The sun was at its height when she awoke and Taura dragged herself from Palmier's grave, wrapping her heart in iron. Her eyes itched of dry salt and dark soil.

She cursed herself for leaving Palmier alone. For hunting far beyond their property. For not hearing the screams.

Their farm was a bloodbath. The bodies of slaughtered animals and streaking sunbaked blood littered the fields. A stinking pile of three of *them*, slain by Palmier's hand, crowded the open door of the cottage. Their thick grey blood congealed in the heat. A trail of it leading away from the house and into the fields.

Taura rolled them onto their backs, studying their armor, checking their weapons, and searching their bags. The stench that hit her on first approach proved her right. Ghouls. Daggers marked with ancient script. Armor more valuable than she'd ever seen on a ghoul.

Fetid creatures beyond life and death. Shambling, violent, ghastly things that shouldn't be there. They stick to the swamps, cemeteries, underground tunnels, and caverns. They populate the darkness in their disease and filth.

A map in one of the bags. A path back from their house, through the rye fields and past the ancient forest, beyond the marsh and out into the desolation beyond. To the realm where cracked black stone is all that exists for aeons until the spires of the sinking mountains and the wretched cities beyond. And beyond that, even, a starting point.

And she knew why they came. With the crumbling of time and the softening of her body and dulling of her mind, Taura should have remained sharper. Leaner. More prepared. But decades passed and she and Palmier fell into each other; fell into a life of growth and renewal and reward. All despite the death and decay and punishment of her life before. But *he* never forgot, even when she let herself.

From a hidden crawlspace behind their bed, she pulled the chest. Her past.

Her future.

The lock was rough and rusted, popping open with a creak. Sandy moth eggs covered the burlap layer beneath. She moved it aside with a plume of grit and dust filling the air of their home. *Her* home. Beneath sat her leather armor. Stained dark with sweat and blood and sun. Flexible but harder than stone, having been treated with layer after layer of cragfox oil and bogshroom wax. Time had worn the vibrancy of its red color, but it remained whole, uncracked, and as expertly fit as when she last took it off. It slipped on easy. As did the pants, arm guards, and boots.

Below that was her axe. The metal was pitted and flaked. Antique blood and bile spent the years eating away at it. Dulling it. Pulling the shine of the metal into oblivion. The handle was flaking away in splinters of fragile driftwood. Salt and moths and fluids and time had reduced it to little else than kindling. A slimy flap of leather hung off it limply. Tarnished by rot and neglect.

She pulled it out, gently at first, before smashing it into the wooden floor of the cottage. The head stuck but the handle snapped, shattering into dozens of shards.

Something else glistened from the bottom of the chest, calling to her. She held it to her face, warmth cascading off it, almost uncomfortable yet perfectly so. It shone in her eyes, the silver black glow of eternity. It was impossible to ignore the sensation of universes dying and birthing within the small antler in her hands. It was deceptively heavy.

She'd forgotten how beautiful it was. How alluring.

How dangerous. How much *he'd* wanted it back.

She remembered Bartok's final words to her. Standing over her battered body, his own dripping with the poison blood of the Swampfox God. She peered into the horn, it was pulling her deeper in. Towards some kind of paradise. Towards all she'd ever wanted. Towards peace and power and hope and freedom. He spit off to the side, shimmering pink like the membrane of a glazseed.

"It ain't what it tells you, that dead god."

Something about the simplicity of his words broke her from her spell. The gentle kindness of a warrior she'd known long enough to trust not just with her life, but with whatever lay beyond. The way his words diffused the antler's power in her mind, grounding her from letting herself go.

It stuck.

Even now, having pulled it from the crate, his words echoed in her mind. His tattered furs and single working eye staring hard at her. Not the harshness of a predator, but the hard-nosed intensity of a long-suffering friend. Telling her exactly what she needed to know in just the right way.

Placing the antler in her leather satchel, she wondered whatever became of Bartok after she left the warrior's life.

Had he survived?

She imagined him old, much like her, perhaps surrounded by children and a patient, loving wife. Maybe fields to plow and crops to barter. Or the owner of a meadhall.

If only we are all so lucky.

Her knees creaked as she stood, the armor suddenly heavier than it had ever been. Shoulders groaning, she grabbed the head of her axe and headed to the barn.

Fashioning a new handle took no time. She'd spent her twilight years building, carving, and creating all manner of wood and bone craft. She even had the right piece for the job.

She pulled the antler from her bag. The fibers were dense and strange, unlike anything she'd ever worked with. It didn't want to flex. It hated being touched like this. She sensed it pulsing off the thing. But all she needed was one point.

Eventually it gave, dense orange fluids oozing from the pores of the cut. Something screamed in her head, but she saved every drop. After hours, her axe had a handle. She polished it over and over with spiketree oil, fenrir wax, and the antler's precious fluid. Before long it shimmered like crystal and was ten times as strong.

The weight of it was right in her hand and she sighed with relief.

Cleaning and honing the blade was another matter, again taking hours. She ground it on the wheel until it split a log with nearly no effort, and then she buffed and shined the metal until the pits and stains were gone. She used the rest of the antler fluid and eventually it was mirror clean. But something shifted in the reflection. Not behind her, not even within her.

Within it.

That same terrible death and rebirth of universes. She held it in her hand and yet it was still in her bag.

It ain't what it tells you, that dead god.

After wrapping the handle with leather and oil treating it, she passed out on a pile of hay—Palmier, the animals, the farm, their life together all tearing through her heart. *They're all gone,* her final thought before she was pulled into a deep, unsettling dream. The weight of the day on her body and mind broke open in her slumber. Still the dripping, crystalline teeth. But also something else. It watched with its strange, orange cervine eyes. It showed her what was to come. The twin moons colliding. A barn owl rotting in a field. A thousand vibrating insects bringing it down to little else than feather and bone. The earth retaking even that, and tiny, unknowable organisms birthed and dying within that tiny world, unaware of us just as we are unaware of the cosmos beyond.

She saw Palmier and the love they had for each other. She saw thousands die at her own hand. The hot blood glistening on her skin in the sunlight and the moonlight and the morning dawn; the blood that soaked into her skin and wouldn't go away even though she couldn't see it any longer. She saw the lives of pain left behind in her wake while she escaped to a life of love and joy. Until now.

It showed her everything. It showed her the end.

Taura woke in a sweaty haze, morning light creeping in through the slats in the walls of the barn she'd constructed decades back. She gathered supplies.

The armor on her back.

The axe in her hand.

The satchel on her hip.

The antler of a dead god.

The map.

A small bundle of food.

Some gold.

Palmier's knife.

And as she walked out from the farm, she imagined returning after one last excursion, everything tied up in a perfect bow, and resuming her life. But she knew it was a lie. There was nothing to return to. Nothing to go to. Nowhere left but blood.

She followed the trail of blood away from the farm,

immediately disregarding the markings on the map. No, she followed the smear of death.

It went for miles though the familiar terrain of the open, dancing rye fields, finally disappearing into the old growth of the forest. She knew the trees well. Had hunted in them plenty of times with her old bow. Glistening grey soaked into a patch of moss near one of her footpaths. This was going to be easy.

She tracked it deeper and deeper into the forest. Far beyond her normal haunt and into areas of dense and strange growth that bordered the swamplands. The air grew humid and heavy. Her joints ached and swelled, and the axe became more difficult to hold onto.

As foul water started to squish beneath her feet, she finally saw him. Yards ahead, on a makeshift path through the vines and dripping trees. His back was to her, and he was slumped in front of a fire. She moved as quickly as she could, never one to betray the silence needed. And then she was atop him, and before she even put thought to mind her axe slid through his neck at an upward angle. There was no resistance. No sound uttered. No moment of shock. His greenish head gently floated in the air before disappearing below the still surface of the swamp water.

The rest of him didn't move.

Taura walked to the other side of his body only then seeing that he was torn open from groin to throat. His freshly open neck a nice flourish to the existing gore running down beneath it. She studied the wound, an ache in her heart trying to open, but she pushed it down, forcing herself to figure out what beast had done it.

Before she could react, the surface of the water broke again, this time followed by a stinking beast with razor claws that reached out to shred Tarua's face. The axe came down, hard, severing the thing's arm which landed on the uneven marsh floor between them. Green slime and clotted blood poured from its wound, and it hissed. For the first time she got a good glance at it.

Hunched but more than seven feet tall. Like an amphibious bat and marshtoad created an unholy alliance of spirit and flesh. An ancient Swampsangui. A primordial demigod. It cried out in a piercing wail and swiped again with its other hand, which bounced off Taura's armor, sending her careening back, almost spilling her into the water. She tried to regain her footing, but the ground was slick with cold mud. Her joints screamed. And then it was on her.

Its slimy, spiked tongue wrapped around her arm, tearing at the flesh. She almost dropped the axe, but wouldn't let it go out of pure desperation of will. Pivoting her body, she tugged them towards each other with the tongue, tossing her weapon in the air with a slight flourish.

The creature creaked and groaned, pulling its other arm back to strike, but it didn't see the damn thing coming. Her axe entered its skull, cracking it like a nut, before it bored into the rest of the beast, cleaving it apart at an odd angle that severed part of the torso from the rest at a downward slash from center of the head to the right side of its hip.

No other sound was uttered but for the impact of the axe and the two sections of its body hitting the wet marsh floor.

Taura breathed for a moment, collected her axe, consulted her map, and was on her way. She was out of the swamp before the light of the next day fell once again and the twin moons met in perfect harmony overhead.

Her bones screamed, but she pressed on, tending to the wounds in her arm each night, morning, and at rest until they had scabbed over in hardened crust, and she was deep into the desolate landscape of the place beyond the swamp.

Sun beat down overhead, cooking the cracked black rock below. Harsh winds danced across the landscape with little sand to push around, mostly just crying a song between the occasional clusters of crumbling ancient stones. Some say this was once a mountain that had been reclaimed by the earth, just as was happening to the mountains on the horizon line. But others claim it was once a vast ocean boiled away by time and an angry sun.

That's what Palmier believed. They believed in the ancient world before. The time that time forgot. And the anger of the elements for being forgotten as gods. They still prayed to the soil. To the plants.

Had.

They *had* prayed to the soil and the plants.

They *had* worshiped at the altar of forces older than words.

And Taura loved them for it. More than ever, so she pressed on in the dehydrating heat, finding just enough life in the crevasses and stone clusters to keep her alive. Her leather armor baked on her back, burning into her flesh. Its dark red stain grew ever darker in the flame. The oils in her axe purged, trickling like boiling honey over her blistered hands.

But she wouldn't stop. Walking day and night until she got to the mountains, which welcomed her like looming gravestones and opened their dark pathways like the crypts of decrepit ghouls. And in those paths, she found life again. The cool shade offered her more than she could have imagined. Not just reprieve, but renewal and hope. Razorblossoms and moon jasmine soothed her crisp-burnt flesh. Small trickles of spring water creeping through miniscule holes in the rocks saturated the cracking skin of her parched lips and throat.

To drink is for the living.

She took one look back at the desolation behind her, a

straight line back from where she came was imprinted on the black stone. We scar the earth with our paths in life. And we ourselves are scarred for it. A lesson from her god.

Tangles of endless paths through the bottom of the sinking mountains eventually progressed upward. Days of a gentle climb on grassy hills grew to jagged stone edges and obstacles. Breaking only for food and small amounts of rest, Taura equally thanked the mountain for saving her from the desolation but also cursed it for being so in the damn way.

She almost fell on several occasions, nearly ending her journey down steep cracks. Eventually, out of breath and deliriously tired, she crossed over one of the smaller peaks. It groaned beneath her, shifting slightly with every step. Sinking back into the earth that had birthed it. As will we all.

Going down was no less tricky, with holes and spiked stone at every step. She steadied herself as she went, thankful for her old boots which had never failed her. Over a week on the mountain and she was at the bottom, breathing in lush air from the golden prairies before her.

There were farms off in the distance, the first signs of life she'd seen since she'd left this place so many years ago. Past those were the cities, small at first before amassing into Rahal, the birthplace of all. Or at least that was their legend. A city built on the ruins of a city built on ruins and so on back and back and back as far as historians could tell. A central point in the history of their time.

Taura walked past the farms and their families. Past the workers in the fields and the small villages full of desperate people and a price tag on everything. She abhorred their systems. The way they ground people into dust just to keep everything moving. They way they silently ran on blood. She hated herself for the way she was a part of that machination. For the way it kept her fed and drunk and full of stories told around campfires with Bartak and other warriors. Laughing and boasting about the misery they'd wrung out into the world. The misery they'd wrung out and smeared around for their own benefit.

She looked the people in the eyes as she passed them in narrow alleyways and through town squares. She carried their burden, just as she had helped forge their pain. And none of them knew. About her. About the secret truth of the whole affair. The way battle was a tool of the rich solely for their benefit lubricated with the blood of the young. The struggling. The innocent.

Taura looked them in the eyes and took in their misery. Accepted it and her place in helping create it. She wouldn't stop, but she would remember. She would press on. Passing towns became villages became cities and eventually she was in Rahal, where she stopped for a meal and to let her swollen feet have a moment to recover.

Sitting down sent lightning down her spine, legs, and into her heels. But the stew was filling and savory and the mead flowed easily. Her spirits never lifted or fell, they simply maintained. There was no rest, there was only the end.

On her fifth mug three men sat down with her. No, not men. Barely boys. They were loud and drunk, assaulting her with questions, wanting to know details of the outer wilds. She ignored them, and eventually they told her to fuck off and left. It was only later, long after they were gone, that she realized her satchel was missing.

With the antler.

She crashed out the door, headed in any direction, hoping to stumble upon them, hoping for any sign of life, but none came. Her head grew heavy as the world spun around her and she collapsed behind an inn in a dark recess of an alley. Her own voice mocked her in her mind.

Lightweight.

She came to in the morning, strained neck and knots in her back from sleeping on jagged rocks. But she was intact.

Figuring the nearest town square was the best place to find it if they'd sold it, she headed out, walking through the entire neighborhood with nary a soul being heard or seen. *Maybe it's just early.* She tried to comfort herself with the thought, but she knew she was wrong.

Town square was empty. But the antler was sitting in the middle of it. Seven new small points had sprouted from the root of the one she had cut. It burned her hand when she touched it and hundreds of voices screamed in her soul, like it had swallowed them.

Taura placed it back in her satchel and continued on, through the rest of the city, into populated areas, and out into the edge of town. Past the lone castle and into the unexplored beyond.

She expected guards or an expansive celestial sky above or a wasteland of electrical storms, but what was beyond the city was simply farms. So, she walked. Past those and into the fields which led to a forest. Ancient in a way that the word doesn't describe.

A forest out of time. Before time. Expansive root structures that tangled into each other creating one single tree organism which choked out any and all new growth that tried to take root. Bodies of animals, travelers, warriors, and royalty knitted within the fibers of the roots. Some fresh, some petrified. Plants so old they had seen empires rise and fall only for new ones to take their place before it all happened over and over and over again.

Primordial.

Everything creaked and moaned and shifted around her, like Taura's body was too young and would taint the place. Off in the darkness there were whispers in tongues she didn't recognize. Tongues she couldn't decipher if they were human or beast or ghoul or tree or stone or something else entirely.

This was the domain of gods long forgotten.

Gods older than iron or stonework or cities or humans or bones or even soil. Gods older than the oceans. It crept up her spine and she shivered. Their eyes were on her. So she kept going.

And at the edge of the primordial forest, she found the beyond. Like walking through a veil.

The sky cracked into sections, waving lights glowing off in the distance of the cosmos. A black star nearly blinded her when she looked into it. Celestial bodies collided and crumbled. New stars were born. New planets broke off from others and circled the fresh orbits of the budding stars. Stars burned out. Planets decayed away into little else than dust.

The ground before her was ancient and volcanic. Shimmering black glass. Before her stood a castle, gnarled and strange. Structurally impossible, bending and shifting like a living being. The antler hummed.

Taura stepped onto the glassy ground, thinking of Palmier. Thanking them for the life they'd created together. Then she walked on. She was halfway to the structure when they arrived, appearing around her.

They of splintered shields, shattered skulls, broken bones, and dried out hearts. Rage in their eyes. The thousand-some dead by her hand. Electricity filled the air for a moment and then they attacked. Taura shielded her head and face, trying her best to parry their blows but she was overrun.

She swung erratically, trying her best to take as many of them with her as she could, but her strikes whiffed through the air, landing on nothing, shedding no blood.

Their blows didn't hurt her flesh; didn't penetrate her organs. They sliced and gouged and split open her soul. A moment of communication between each of them and her. Their pain became her pain. She breathed their final breaths, watched behind their eyes as the lights went dim and the only thoughts left were about spouses and children and parents and siblings and friends and monumental failures and regrets and unattained hopes and dreams. The moment of cold unknown. That moment of true loneliness.

It ripped through her. Each successive blow, another's anguish and loss. Hours passed before they were through with her. And when they were, very little remained inside. They had hollowed her out. And then they vanished.

She still saw their eyes. The hatred. The venom. The pain. Their eyes wouldn't leave. But she crawled toward the castle, dragging her axe along as she went. She couldn't breathe right. She couldn't steady herself. She pressed on until the black glass crested up, meeting the porous surface of the shifting monument.

Forcing herself onto her feet, she reached into her bag and pulled out the antler. No longer like that of a normal deer, but crystal in her hand. Vibrating, torturously hot, swirling universes born and dead inside; their movements matching the primordial sky above.

She touched the crystal antler to the castle and the world froze.

Then *he* was there. Staring through her. Everything gone dark but for a single dying black star above flickering off and on and alive and dead. The final cries of a body more ancient than the ground she stood upon.

He moved to her, slithering movements like a serpent despite *his* long legs and cloven hooves. Crystal liquid dripped from *his* perfectly razor teeth. Like a deer but not a deer. No longer made from blood and fur and muscle and bone and fat. Now sharp crystal, universes writhing inside. Perfect, but for *his* one missing antler.

As *he* got closer, Taura thought her skin might blister and boil from the heat. As confidently as she could, she raised her axe and struck down on *his* neck with everything she had left. *He* didn't shatter. Didn't crack. Didn't chip.

Like her axe simply stopped on impact. No rebound. No bounceback. Like it was sinking into dense liquid.

She lifted it and struck again and again and again, smashing the blade against every possible part of *him* until she no longer had the strength to swing it. Her body broken down and her spirit left in tatters. She forced herself to strike again, to kill the horrible beast; to find justice or vengeance or relief. Sweat poured from her brow as she raised the axe. But her grip was beyond fatigue and the axe slipped from her hand, hitting the ground below, severing into the glass before it stopped with an echoing crack as she gasped for air. Her muscles trembled under her weight.

He looked up at her with his cervine eyes and turned *his* head, revealing the hole where *his* antler once was. *He* was asking.

But this wasn't what she was here for. She pulled out Palmier's dagger and thrust it down into the hole where the antler had been. Pressing all her weight, struggling to hold on, it sunk in slowly, like stabbing hard-packed dirt. *He* didn't react; *he* only looked at her with the question.

Bartok's words rushed back into her mind. *It ain't what it tells you, that dead god.*

The knife came out easy, dripping with the miasma glowing black fluid of dying universes. Taura returned it to her satchel and stared into *his* eyes. Still simply the question.

She lifted the antler and placed it back into the fissure. *He* was whole. And then she was alone again. In the beyond. No more castle, just mocking celestial bodies staring down at her, and an endless expanse ahead of her.

Taura looked back, her stygian reflection stretching along the path she had come. For a moment, she considered going back home. But she had no reason to. There was no home anymore.

Her muscles screamed as she picked up her axe and walked deeper into the beyond. Above her, the twin moons met, becoming one.

ABOUT THE AUTHORS

Emma Alice Johnson grows wildflowers and writes. She lives on a farm dedicated to conservation of native plants and endangered insects. She has released a number of zines, chapbooks, micro press and art press novellas. Her short fiction has appeared in more than 75 publications. When she isn't planting or writing, she can be found running through the woods with her pet pig, singing to her chickens, lifting weights, watching B-movies or reading while snuggled with her cat. Learn more at www.freaktension.com.

After self-publishing zines and Comix for a long while, **Adam Smith** released *Long Walk to Valhalla* with Matt Fox on Archaia/Boom! In 2015. Since then, he has worked with Lion Forge, Oni, Boom!, and The Jim Henson Company gathering an Eisner, Harvey, and Gem Award nomination while appearing on The New York Public Library's Best New Comics For Adults. He has recently started to meander into prose with publications from Castaigne Publishing, Bag of Bones Press, and Close to the Bone Publishing.

Matthew Mitchell is a fiction and comics writer from the Ozarks. His debut novella CHAINDEVILS received the Literary Nasties Award and his short fiction has been published in various anthologies, including the award-winning VOID HAUS. Matthew's comics have appeared in Heavy Metal Magazine and he is co-editor of the HORRORIUM comics anthology.

Sara Century is a horror creator across many mediums, including but not limited to podcasts, short stories, zines, photography, and critical essays. She is the author of the short story collection *A Small Light & Other Stories* through Weirdpunk as well as heading up the Decoded Horror Channel and Medusa Mask podcasts. She's always up to something so check for updates at saracentury.com.

Charles Austin Muir is a writer, personal trainer, and widower living in Portland, Oregon. He is the author of *Slippery When Metastasized* and the Splatterpunk Award-nominated *This Is a Horror Book*. He also wrote a children's book, *Pug Monster Gallery*, in collaboration with his wife and illustrator, Kara Picante Muir. His short film, *A History of Worry*, based on his experiences as a cancer caregiving spouse, won the Oregon Short Film Festival's Best Experimental Micro Film Award.

Edwin Callihan resides in the foothills of Appalachia. He will probably die there. He also writes weird fiction and watches a lot of television. *Histories Of Mgo* is his first short story collection.

Sam Richard is the author of a few books, including *Grief Rituals* and *Sabbath of the Fox-Devils*. *Profane Altars* is the tenth anthology he's edited. His short fiction litters the literary wasteland in various anthologies and magazines and he has been nominated for several awards and even won two. Widowed in 2017, he slowly rots in Minneapolis where he runs Weirdpunk Books. You can stalk him @SammyTotep across socials or at weirdpunkbooks.com.

Infinity Mathing at the Shore & Other Disruptions - M. Lopes da Silva

A heartfelt, disquieting collection of short stories focused on body horror, transness, anti-capitalism, queerness, decay, transformation, living buildings, rot, ruin, vintage arcade games, and so much more. With *Infinity Mathing at the Shore & Other Disruptions*, M. Lopes da Silva has solidified themself as an essential and sharp voice in the canon of 21st century queer horror.

Cover art by legendary punk artist Croad.

Feral Architecture: Ballardian Horrors - edited by Sam Richard

J.G. Ballard has held a tremendous influence on culture since he first started writing, much of which turned out to be prophetic. In *Feral Architecture* Joe Koch, Donyae Coles, Sara Century, Brendan Vidito, and editor Sam Richard plume the depth of that influence through the lens of horror fiction.

The results are surreal, ominous, unexpected, unnerving, and a fitting tribute to the legacy of one of the 20th century's most impactful and important writers.

Featuring a foreword by Scott Dwyer of The Plutonian.

Elogona - Samantha Kolesnik

An evocative tale of sapphic love in a post-apocalyptic world dominated by religious zealots and supernatural monsters.

Kolesnik's *Elogona* transports readers to a time after the world's end, when a long-dormant sea creature has awoken to stake its claim against one of the last human settlements.

Verna must battle both man and monster to protect her family and her newfound love for Audrey, a refugee from the mainland.

Meanwhile, the Elogona calls…

"Otherworldly and grounded, immersive and gut-wrenching, *Elogona* feels all too real."

— RAE KNOWLES (*MERCILESS WATERS*)